AF506794

BOURBON
· PENN ·

32

March 2024

CONTENTS

HEATHMAN LDG

———— ■ ————

Brian Evenson

His final jaunt, just before he dropped off the map entirely, Erlend spent weeks without going home, traveling from town to town, staying at hotel after hotel, taking his sample books and displaying them to whatever merchants he found loaded into his itinerary each day. The company had, in the past, always given him a few days off every week or two, and had also set his schedule so those days would fall at a time when his route brought him close to home. But perhaps either a new person was scheduling him now, or there had been some sort of not-yet diagnosed computer glitch, or the company had changed policies in ways that were not completely legible and that he couldn't understand. Still, what did it matter? His wife had left him a few months before, and they had never had children, nor pets: he had no one to go home to.

And yet, it did matter. That many days on the road, that many days in a row, and you started to lose track of yourself. Most mornings Erlend woke up unsure what town he was in, disoriented, confused. And whenever he picked up his phone, it seemed like the company's app told him where he was to go next, not where he was. He was living away from what he thought of as his real life and, in this new false life, was always unsure of where he was at any given moment, always freed to look ahead to the town to come.

There were strange echoes too, even if these were mostly false. Moments when he would recognize the town name that appeared on the company app, *Lancaster* for instance, and think he was going back to a place he had already been, only to later that day arrive in a town that wasn't familiar at all. One part of his mind recognized that of course more than one town could have the same name: there might be a town called Lancaster, for instance, in every state within his territory, not to mention the states outside it. But another, growing part of him was more and more concerned. It didn't seem right how often he recognized a town name only to arrive there and find it not at all the town he had anticipated. It was as if something had been offered to him, and then, before he could claim it, been yanked away.

He awoke one morning, late in his jaunt, to a message from the company. *Next stop*, it read, *Lancaster*. But he was, he was sure, almost sure, in Lancaster already. He refreshed the app: same thing. *Next stop, Lancaster.*

All right, then. Lancaster it was. *No problem*, the rational side of his mind kept insisting: many towns had the same name. It was mere coincidence that he would be in two Lancasters in a row—if that really was the case: was he absolutely sure the town he was in now was called Lancaster? Maybe Lancaster had been the day before, or even the day before that. Days tended to blur more and more for him now, but to acknowledge this did not particularly reassure him.

He checked the time. He'd slept late, had to hustle. He rummaged a stale granola bar out of his bag, ate it while getting dressed, then hurried down to his car.

Did I check out? he wondered from the driver's seat. He wasn't sure, but wouldn't they have stopped him if he hadn't? They could email him a bill if need be. Before leaving the lot, he entered the coordinates for the hotel in Lancaster: Heathman Lodge. The car map started to chart the path and then froze: the path to reach the hotel was there, but the last dozen miles or so were blank: no road, no indications of houses or infrastructure or landscape: only a blue dot in the middle of nowhere labeled *Heathman Ldg. The map's just not loading,* he told himself, and started driving anyway: he was already late. But even after an hour on the road, that last little bit of the map still remained empty and blank: the only thing within it was the blue dot labeled *Heathman Ldg.*

He stopped for gas. A trucker's diner was attached to the gas station and he grabbed a quick lunch there: patty melt, limp fries. When he started the car again, the map image still came up incomplete. He turned the car off, restarted it again. Same result. He entered the coordinates into his phone, but even on that map it was the same: a series of empty quadrants with the blue *Heathman Ldg* dot floating in the middle.

Glitch, he told himself. *Or maybe they simply haven't mapped it yet.* There were those cars that went around with cameras strapped to their roofs, photographing road after road, but maybe they hadn't gotten to Lancaster yet—*this* Lancaster anyway. Surely there were places like that, places not quite fully on a digital map yet. But even as he thought this, he realized he didn't quite believe it.

He turned off the car and went back into the gas station.

"Something the matter?" the attendant asked.

"Car map's not working," Erlend said. "Do you have a paper one?"

"Paper map?" The attendant pursed her lips, shook her head. "No real call for one these days. Where you trying to get to?" And then, when Erlend explained: "Lancaster? Can't say I know it."

It was, at least according to his car map, still more than an hour away, so maybe it was plausible, just barely, that the attendant wouldn't know it. Erlend thanked her and left.

The road didn't end exactly, but it didn't exactly continue either. There, just at the point where the car map became blank, the asphalt abruptly stopped, replaced by a packed dirt road. *This can't be right,* he thought. He put the car into park and stared.

A wide dirt road, carefully attended to. It led up a gentle hill covered in tall, shivering grass, then slipped over the top of it.

He got out his phone and opened the company's app, entered the coordinates again. It took longer than before, but eventually the same map loaded, with the same blankness, the same blue dot, the same words: *Heathman Ldg.*

He stared a little longer, thinking. After a moment, not knowing what else to do, he put the car into gear and drove.

It was not a bad road, was nearly as good as the asphalt one. Maybe, he told himself, this was a new town, an intentional community, just developed. That could explain the dirt road. It might explain the problem with the map as well. He climbed the hill and passed over the top of it. On the other side was a gentle slope down and then another hill. Past that was, as it turned out, another downslope, followed by another hill. No sign of habitation, no houses, nothing but this solitary dirt road cutting its way across hill after hill.

Someone at the company must be having a joke at his expense. Either that or something was truly wrong.

He went up and down another hill, then another. He was beginning to feel psychically seasick. *Should I turn around?* he wondered. But if he turned around, where would he go? This was his assignment. If he wanted to keep his job, was there any other choice but to keep going?

He was on the verge of stopping and going back when he saw, at the top of the next hill, a green metal sign with white lettering. It was too far away for him to read. He drove toward it, squinting, but it wasn't until he was nearly there that he realized it read,

LANCASTER

Pop.

Population what? Erlend wondered. No number was listed. The sign looked brand new, as if it hadn't spent even a full day out in the sun. He slowly passed it, reached the top of the hill and there, on the other side, in the middle of nowhere, he saw Lancaster.

• • •

It was a small town, hard to judge exactly how many people from the ridge. Four hundred, perhaps. Maybe five. There was a gate at the town's edge, open, that he could drive through, a central street with a few shops, glimpses of several side streets studded with seemingly identical houses, but that was about all. His map still showed that he was in the middle of nothing, but it still led him, inexorably, to the blue dot labeled *Heathman Ldg*.

Lancaster was strange. It seemed new, for one thing, as if it might have been thrown together quickly, in a day. There were, too, no cars to be seen: his was the only one. And there were no people to be seen, not a one—even when he peered into the shop windows while driving by he saw absolutely nothing but blank, carefully arranged surfaces. No sign of human presence or, even, sign that humans had ever been inside. It was as if he had wandered into a movie set.

The car map informed him he had arrived. He pulled to the curb, switched off the vehicle. There it was, Heathman Lodge, a midblock red brick edifice with an empty fountain stationed before it. He climbed out and took his bag out of the trunk and, making a wide circle around the dry fountain, went inside.

The lobby had a fountain as well, also dry. The walls were paneled in planks of reclaimed and lightly lacquered pine. The front desk consisted of a huge slab of polished knotty pine with a natural edge, resting on two squat and rusty metal pillars.

Nobody was standing behind the desk. Nobody, in fact, was in the lobby at all. Except, that is, for him. There was a bell. He dinged it, waited. When nobody came, he dinged it again. He was preparing to ding it a third time when he noticed, in a metal outbox in one corner of the desk, a key with a label affixed to it. He sidled down the slab for a closer look, and saw that the label had a room number on it, and the name *Erlend*.

333 his room number was. *Halfway to the devil*, he thought absurdly. He took the key, called the elevator. The third was the top floor—the elevator didn't go any higher. He depressed 3 and waited for the doors to slide closed.

When they opened again, he pushed his way out. The hall was just as empty as the lobby had been, as if except for him the hotel was deserted. He began counting his way to his room.

There was something about the hall, something strange, something he was hearing that he shouldn't be. Was there a bird loose? And then he realized it was coming from a speaker, that bird noises were being piped in. He had started off in one direction and only when he was standing between 332 and 334 did he realize that all the rooms around him, no matter which side of the hall they were on, were even numbers. He backtracked to the elevator and went the other direction, the bird noises growing, then receding, then growing again. There, at last, it was: 333. He slid the key in and the door clicked open.

It was, in all important respects, an ordinary room. Nothing surprising: a pair of twin beds; a dark pressed wood desk and matching cabinet; a picture of a sunset bought, perhaps, somewhere in bulk and to be found, perhaps, in all the rooms; a bathroom that looked as though it had never been used.

He put his bag on the luggage rack, removed the toiletries from it, balanced them on the edge of the sink. He slid his laptop out of his briefcase, sat at the desk, and tried to connect with the WiFi.

There was a WiFi connection, *Heathman Lodge*, but to use it he had to enter a code. He looked at the back of the label attached to the key: no instructions, no code. *Maybe it was on a slip of paper and I dropped it,* he thought, though this seemed doubtful. He looked around the room for something that would list the WiFi code. Nothing. He opened the desk and cabinet drawers, but they were empty.

He picked up the phone, dialed. It rang three times, then was picked up.

"Hello?" he said. "Can I get the wireless code?" And when nobody responded, "Hello? Hello?"

The line went dead. Had there ever been anybody there at all? Was it just an answering machine with its message erased? He tried calling back. This time, no answer.

He turned off his laptop's WiFi receiver, turned it on again, then waited for a few minutes as it scanned for joinable networks. There it was again, *Heathman Lodge*, the little lock next to it insisting he couldn't connect without the code. Then another network popped onto the list: *Heathman Ldg*, spelled as it had been on the map app, next to the blue dot. No lock icon next to it. He clicked on it and was almost immediately connected.

• • •

But something was odd about his screen. Power surge, maybe. It flickered, offered little bursts of static. He opened his company app, clicked on the tab with his appointments schedule, but instead of displaying the calendar his screen grew dim. He leaned in, peered closely. There was, just visible, a faint image of a circle on it, though not exactly a circle. He didn't know if there was a word for the shape he was seeing. It was how a circle would look if it were alive and had a mouth. And an eye: it seemed to be watching him.

He reached very slowly toward the laptop, planning to close it without startling the circle that was not a circle. He had just touched the lid when the image changed. Three wavy lines now, vertically arranged, spooning one another—or no, four lines. No, three. No, five? Lines anyway, somehow three and four and five of them all at once. He tried to look away but found he could not. He groaned. And then the lines turned, all at once, and they were not lines at all but something vibrating with a music which was not of a frequency that he could actually hear but that he could feel buzzing on his skin.

• • •

He woke up hours later, still dressed, the laptop in front of him now dead. He was not sure exactly how much time had passed. Was it morning already? The sample books were scattered about on the bed, many of the samples removed and crumpled or torn. His head ached, and when he moved his eyes they felt like they were scraping against their sockets.

He closed the laptop and slipped it back into his briefcase. He stood up, went into the bathroom, looked into the mirror. His face was pale, drawn, as if he hadn't slept. Perhaps he hadn't. He steadied himself on the lip of the bathroom sink. What could he remember? Very little, vague memories, dreams maybe. His toiletries, he saw, had been emptied into the bathtub, the open bottles lying near the drain, webbed in dried foam. Had he done that?

He could remember the sound of someone at the door and the door opening and the noise of birds, but birds louder than he remembered the speakers in the hall being. A dream surely. And someone or something, several someones or somethings, in the room with him, and, even louder now, the noise of birds, the language of birds. His shirt was dotted here and there with something: fire mites he thought at first, dozens or even hundreds of them, but when he tried to brush them off nothing happened. He washed and dried his glasses and then moved closer to the mirror and saw they weren't mites at all, but a blown mist of blood.

His mouth was very dry. He turned on the sink, lapped water from it like a dog, like an animal of some sort anyway. He washed his face. That was a little better. Not much, but a little. He was hungry, he realized. When had he last eaten? He returned to the bedroom and rifled through his bag. One last granola bar, at the very bottom, mostly crushed. He ate the broken chunks, shook the dust into his mouth, then took out his phone.

Already 9:30. He was running late. Time to go. But he hadn't done anything here, hadn't met with any merchants, hadn't turned in his nightly report. He had let the company down. Surely that would mean he'd have to stay here another night. Where was here again?

But when he opened the company app he found a banner he hadn't seen before. *Congratulations!* it said. Because of his diligence he was being chosen to represent a new product line to a new clientele base. A series of new sample books would be waiting for him in the next town.

· · ·

For a few minutes he just held his head in his hands, then quickly he packed everything and headed out. The hall was just as deserted as it had been the afternoon before, no sound except for the piped-in bird noises. The elevator opened immediately when he touched the button. The lobby was deserted. He'd never paid, he realized. He dinged the bell, then dinged it again, but nobody came. Maybe the company had handled it for him? After all, he had been left a key under his name. He dinged again and shouted hello, but finally he left the key in the box and went out.

His car was still the only car. The shops still looked empty. He climbed in and opened the company app and looked at where he was going.

Next stop, it read, *Lancaster*.

Lancaster, he thought. He reached for the key, then stopped. Hadn't he just been in Lancaster? He shook his head. He felt dazed, hadn't gotten nearly enough sleep. The company had been running him ragged. He needed to call someone, ask for a few days off. But he could hardly do that right when he'd been promoted, could he?

He entered the coordinates for Lancaster into his phone. A path appeared on his car's map screen, leading to the hotel he'd be staying at. The name sounded familiar.

Must be a chain, he told himself. He must have stayed there before.

Something was wrong with the map: it wasn't filling in. Where he currently was remained blank except for the red arrow that was his car. And where he was going was blank as well, except for the blue dot marked *Heathman Ldg.*

Putting the car into gear, he drove.

■

Brian Evenson is the author of a dozen and a half books of fiction, most recently None of You Shall Be Spared *(2023) from Weird House Books. A new collection,* Good Night, Sleep Tight *will be published in September of 2024 by Coffee House Press. His work has won the World Fantasy Award, the International Horror Guild Award, and the Shirley Jackson Award, and has been a finalist for the Ray Bradbury Prize. He lives in Valencia, California and teaches at CalArts.*

A TURTLE IN LOVE, SINGING

Tara Campbell

Green Lake Police have received multiple reports of a disgruntled pelican or pelicans loitering in the southeast area of the lake, near the public restrooms.

The pelican in question is larger than average: witnesses describe a white bird about the size of an emu with a bright yellow bucket-beak fixed in a scowl and prominent black eyebrows scrunched into a frown. It is unclear whether there are multiple pelicans, or one pelican is being observed on multiple occasions.

The cause of the pelican's annoyance is yet to be determined, so citizens are advised to avoid the area until further notice. Should you encounter a giant disgruntled pelican, do not look directly at it. Alter your path to avoid it, but don't turn your back on the avian interloper, as this will trigger its attack response. Citizens are advised to keep an eye on small children and pets.

If you encounter a disgruntled pelican(s), please contact the Green Lake Police immediately.

Green Lake Police are monitoring the growth of a small number of carnivorous plants, similar in appearance to the fictional plant Audrey in the Broadway musical and movie "Little Shop of Horrors." There are five plants occupying a ten-foot radius behind the Woodland Park Lawn Bowling Club.

Carnivorous plants are normally not dangerous to humans (see: Venus flytrap, pitcher plants, etc), but these plants have been observed lunging toward dogs that sniff too close. No pets have been harmed thus far, but Scout Troop #4417 has documented an unusually large amount of squirrel bones in the vicinity of the plants.

Citizens are advised to keep pets and small children away from this area until further notice. DO NOT attempt to remove the plants, as that triggers their gag reflex, resulting in the release of spores that produce new specimens. The current colony of five is being monitored, but citizens are asked to contact Green Lake Police if they notice any specimens growing in other areas.

Green Lake Police have received reports of a lion leaning against a naked woman in a shady glade on the side of Green Lake Park where the turtles congregate, that part you notice looks so nice and cool toward the end of your walk around the lake on a hot day. The lion has been described as light brown with a dark brown mane and a calm demeanor. Witnesses have thus far not seen any indication that the woman has been harmed or is presently in danger. To repeat: no one has been harmed, no one appears to be in danger. Citizens are advised to stay clear and just let them have their moment. There is no need to keep calling the Green Lake Police about this unless the situation changes.

Green Lake Police have received reports of an elephant talking to a fallen leaf under a weeping bottlebrush tree at the northernmost tip of the lake. It is currently autumn, so a fallen leaf is not suspicious. The elephant appears to be calm. The topic of discussion between the elephant and the leaf is as yet unclear. The one witness who got close enough to listen reported hearing the word "lion" from the leaf, and something about a "shark" from the elephant before the elephant trumpeted and stomped in the direction of the witness. As previously advised in similar situations, citizens are asked to stay clear and just let them have their privacy. Please do not approach to eavesdrop, and refrain from calling Green Lake Police about this incident unless the situation changes.

———

Green Lake Police have received reports of a shark breaching the surface of Green Lake. Sightings began yesterday, and peaked around sunset, bringing to mind the leaping dolphins in Florida that make the place look like an honest-to-God Lisa Frank Trapper Keeper.

All swimming, boating, paddleboarding, etc is prohibited in Green Lake until further notice. Please do not attempt to hunt the shark, no matter what you have heard about its intent here in Green Lake or how strongly you feel the desire to re-enact "Jaws." Do not entertain rumors that it is searching for the woman and the lion, despite the viral video where it reportedly surfaces and shouts, "They have blighted the empire of sharks and thus vengeance must be mine!"

The woman and the lion have been conducted to an undisclosed location for their safety. As far as we are aware, sharks cannot live or hunt on land, despite the suggestion of 1970s-era late night comedy sketches, but citizens who see any evidence to the contrary are asked to contact Green Lake Police.

———

Green Lake Police have received reports of a rainbow pegasus unicorn in the vicinity of the Bathhouse Theater. Green Lake Police asked if this was perhaps in conjunction with a current theater production, but were informed that the current production was "The Crucible," and that, though the theater company in question was in favor of modernization and experimental theater, this majestic mythical mash-up was not part of their production.

Officers sent to investigate were only mildly disappointed to find that the intriguingly improbable creature was, in fact, not a pegasus, nor a unicorn, but an inflatable personal raft floating on the lake. Officers did report, however, that the rainbow description only applied to certain sections of the floatation device, and on the whole, the design was a rather more pink-forward affair.

Officers also reported that the passengers in the flotation device were none other than the lion leaning against the nude woman. They attempted to hail the passengers to warn them of the shark sighting, but to no avail. The woman lowered a turtle off the raft into the water, before paddling the raft away across the lake.

At 6:05 this morning Green Lake Police responded to reports of a disturbance behind the Woodland Park Lawn Bowling Club, where they found a large, disgruntled pelican in a tussle with a carnivorous plant over a fish. Officers deescalated the situation by donating a ham sandwich to the contested meal offering. Both the bird and the plant were captured as they digested, and will be delivered to the Washington Department of Fish and Wildlife and the King County Noxious Weed Control Board (KCNWCB), respectively, during normal business hours.

Citizens are advised to stay clear of the area, as there are still more carnivorous plants in the vicinity. KCNWCB is already aware of the situation, citing insufficient personnel as the reason the rest of them have not yet been cleared. They stress that, as valued as citizen scientists are, only trained professionals should attempt to clear the area.

As yet it is still unclear whether there are more pelicans in the area, or if this was the only one. Citizens are advised to be vigilant when holding fish or ham sandwiches in the vicinity of Green Lake.

Shortly after midnight last night, a seven-foot-tall raven with a broken wing entered Green Lake Police Headquarters to report that the Bathhouse Theater had sunk into the lake. Upon hearing dispatch call for officers to report to the theater, the raven became agitated, cawing and flapping, stating that all he needed was a case number and asking why they had to send anyone there, why they didn't believe him at his word.

The desk officer attempted to calm the raven, assuring him that this was standard protocol and had nothing to do with anyone deeming a raven a disreputable witness. Here the desk officer might have overstepped a bit by bringing Raven's trickster reputation into the discussion, even if simply to deny that it played a role. Green Lake Police leadership has taken note of our insufficient protocols for working with mythical members of the public. Green Lake Police leadership hopes that this can be a teachable moment, and promises that new protocols will be crafted at the regional level, in conjunction with tribal representatives, who would likely have used a more appropriate word than "mythical" in this alert.

Without casting aspersions on ravens in general, members of the public are advised not to engage with this particular seven-foot, broken-winged raven. Green Lake Police wish to stress that we by no means believe that all ravens are tricksters. Unfortunately, however, this particular raven does not appear to be trustworthy. After leaving police headquarters in a huff, he swooped repeatedly over squad cars, presumably attempting to deter them from surveying the damage he'd reported. As he battled the cruisers, several sheets of paper slipped from his talons and stuck to the windshield of one of them, obscuring officers' vision. Ultimately, he wasn't able to keep officers from arriving at the theater to find that no damage had, in fact, occurred. The theater had not slipped into the lake. It was instead resting where it had always been, on shore, closed up, darkened for the evening, and resting contentedly after an evening of use.

Further investigation revealed that the raven in question is a half owner of the theater, and the paper he let drop while seeking to delay our investigation turned out to be partially completed paperwork for an insurance claim he may have been planning to submit. Upon questioning, his partner in the theater venture admitted that the theater was not making money—had indeed lost quite a bit of it—which was the subject of an argument he and the raven had had earlier that day.

The raven is sought for questioning regarding potential insurance fraud. Anyone who sees him is advised *not* to engage, as ravens do remember faces and may retaliate. Instead, report the time and location to Green Lake Police immediately, and we will send masked officers out to intercept.

Green Lake Police advises the public to beware of a disgruntled pelican in the area of Green Lake. The pelican escaped from police custody on the way to the Department of Fish and Wildlife, and should be considered hungry and dangerous.

The carnivorous plant with which the pelican was initially apprehended has been safely delivered to the King County Noxious Weed Control Board. Public are advised, however, that only two of the additional weeds near the Woodland Park Lawn Bowling Club have been safely removed. More carnivorous plants are still out there and should be avoided.

Green Lake Police have received reports of a demon frog diva with a heart floating free in her torso. The diva frog was reported in the Taiga Wetlands area near Duck Island. When asked what made this frog a "demon" and a "diva," and how they could see her heart, witnesses responded,

"We don't know, but her cover of 'Sandcastles' slaps." With only one of three questions answered, dispatch sent officers to investigate.

It was a crisp, cool, autumn night, just past 11:00 p.m., when officers parked in the West Green Lake lot. As soon as they stepped out of their vehicle, officers heard a croaky yet eerily beautiful rendition of "My Heart Will Go On." As officers entered the park, trees blocked the illumination of the streetlights, casting their path in inky blackness. A light wind rustled leaves that, in daytime, would be blazing in various stages of green, yellow, orange and red but were, at night, merely undulating blobs of darkness.

Officers followed the aural ache of remembered love onto the public dock, where they saw a glimmer of red seemingly floating above the water. After donning protective earplugs, officers stepped onto the dock leading out toward a throbbing crimson light ebbing and glowing, ebbing and glowing in the night. Officers reported how an ambient halo of red rippled in the breeze on the surface of the lake, how the light was orb-like and pulsing, how it was encased in something larger—something darker— except for the clear view afforded by some sort of window. They reported that the shape holding the orb became clearer as they approached, taking on the outlines of a giant frog floating in lotus position above the lake.

Officers reported that the frog's throat expanded and contracted as it croaked out its tune. At the risk of enchantment, one officer momentarily popped out an earplug, ascertaining that the suspect had indeed segued smoothly into "How Do I Live Without You," even though thematically it might have made more sense to put those two songs in reverse order, upon which the other officer asked, "Exactly what is she 'suspected' of, aside from nailing Celine's high E flat 5 like a pro?" to which the dispatcher replied, "It's just a sighting at this point, officers. No one's a suspect yet. Let's not jump the g— I mean, jump to conclusions."

Officers observed the singing demon frog from the end of the dock while it cycled through "Memory" and "I Dreamed a Dream," prompting a discussion of how "Cats" specifically influenced "Les Mis," aside from its overarching influence on musical theater, all disparagement against it notwithstanding.

Officers observed that the throbbing orb of light inside the frog was, in fact, its heart, and that it was powerful and luminous, and far more beautiful than the gelatinous blobs they'd each carved out of formaldehyde frogs in high school biology.

Officers observed that the eyes of the frog glowed like embers, and smoke curled silkily out of its nostrils. They observed the arms—the front legs—of the frog reaching slowly toward them, sticky palms open, padded fingers splayed, ready to receive.

Officers observed that if not for the dampening effect of the earplugs and the weight of their uniforms (both figuratively and literally), and the oddly loud *bloop* of a turtle slipping into the water, and the voice of their dispatcher yelling for them to stop clogging up the police radio with chatter about power ballads, they would likely have abandoned everything else in their lives to jump off the dock and swim after the demon frog diva with her heart floating free in her torso.

Citizens are advised to stay away from the Taiga Wetlands area of Green Lake until further notice.

<hr>

Green Lake Police responded to a report of a malignant pink blob oozing up onto the eastern shore of Green Lake near the pickleball courts. Outfitted in hazmat suits, officers ascertained that the pink blob was not a biological life form, but rather the deflated remains of a rainbow pegasus flotation device, most likely the same one in which the woman and the lion had earlier been spotted.

Aside from a tuft of fur and a muddy footprint on the shore, there was no sign of either the woman or the lion. Anyone who sees them is advised to leave them be and call Green Lake Police.

Green Lake Police have received reports of a seven-foot-raven in conversation with a girl in a hooded red cloak. They are suspected of rewriting folk stories. Anyone with information is requested to contact Green Lake Police immediately so we know which versions to tell our children at bedtime.

Green Lake Police have received reports of a disgruntled pelican diving after a shark in the southern end of the lake. Officers arrived just as the pelican scooped the shark out of the water. Off balance, the pelican—no longer disgruntled, but somewhat overtaxed—tumbled into the remaining patch of carnivorous plants next to the Woodland Park Lawn Bowling Club. Only by surrendering half the shark was the pelican able to waddle off with its life.

The King County Noxious Weed Control Board (KCNWCB) has received emergency state funding, and National Guard reservists have been called up to assist in the eradication of the rest of the plants.

Citizens are advised to give them their space until further notice.

Green Lake Police have been notified of the return of the demon frog diva with a turtle associate, now in the vicinity of the Bathhouse Theater, which has recently begun an actual, quantifiable slide into the lake. The seven-foot raven, whose wing has healed nicely, has spent the morning plucking letters out of a tray to update the billboard with the theater's newest act. Because ravens are horrible spellers, however, officers have not yet been able to determine the name of the production.

The co-owner of the theater notified officers that they are working on permits for a pontoon system to keep the theater, literally and figuratively, afloat.

Citizens are advised to avoid the area. Green Lake Police will notify the public when the raven has finally pieced together an intelligible name for the new show.

Green Lake Police have received reports of a lion walking alongside a woman riding an elephant holding a leaf in its trunk. The party has left the park and is heading north along 5th Avenue NE, presumably to avoid I-5. There is no need to call police, as they are being monitored. Citizens are advised not to approach or otherwise engage them. They are safe. What more could anyone want?

Green Lake Police have received reports of a disgruntled pelican returning to the Woodland Park Lawn Bowling Club, where the patch of carnivorous plants has been reduced to one remaining specimen. King County Noxious Weed Control Board (KCNWCB) specialists report that the pelican has repeatedly chased off any humans attempting to approach the last plant specimen, disrupting their efforts to eliminate it.

Furthermore, the Department of Fish and Wildlife has ascertained that the pelican in question is indeed just the one bird, rather than multiple birds approaching individually at different times. As such, the Green Lake Disgruntled Pelican has now been designated a protected species.

The National Guard reinforcements have thus been relieved of duty. Any troops that remain on site are there in an unofficial capacity, on their own time, having developed an affinity for birdwatching.

The now-protected Green Lake Disgruntled Pelican has established its nesting area near the carnivorous plant, to which it has been observed delivering one fish per day from the lake. Off-duty National Guard troops report that the pelican actually carries in two fish per day: one for the plant, and one for itself. Once the fish are shared, bird and plant sit quietly together, digesting in companionable silence.

Citizens untrained in the art of birdwatching or carnivorous plant husbandry are advised not to approach the area. Anyone disrupting the nesting area will be fined two fish per day for a length of time to be determined jointly by the Department of Fish and Wildlife and the KCNWCB.

Green Lake Police advises citizens that there is no need to keep reporting the sunken Bathhouse Theater to the police. We are aware that it has slid halfway into the lake. Despite the original plans for pontoons not having been realized, the owners are still pleased at its progress.

Officers observed the seven-foot-raven and the girl in the red cloak poring over a script, the raven bobbing his head and cawing, the girl at times nodding and adding notation, and at other times shaking her head and explaining why not. Further questioning revealed that the girl has bought out the other co-owner, and is now co-owner and playwright for the new Subaquatic Playhouse, a development corroborated by the new sign being hung by a turtle with a wrench.

Somewhere within the half of the theater still on land, a pianist pounded out a strident rendition of "Non, je ne regrette rien" while a woman in a tutu danced, teetering, on the canted spine of the roof.

"We should be ready to open in another two weeks," reported the red-hooded girl. "Once the theater has fully sunk and settled on the lakebed. Imagine it: there, below an unbroken surface, a wide path leading to an open stage. There, as a heavy curtain is unhooked and floats away, a demon frog diva levitates above a stage, her crimson heart beating."

The turtle finished hanging the sign, then dropped the wrench on the shore before sliding down the awning and slipping under the waves.

"With each beat of her heart," said the girl, "the demon frog diva pushes a current of water, pulsing her passion out into the audience. And there, before her, stands the object of her affection—nay, her passion, her devotion—harmonizing with her every note.

"His voice is surprisingly deep," she added. "It's his shell. It's bigger than it seems. He has this way of sneaking up on you, even though he's been there the whole time."

The raven flapped up to the sign and perched, caressing the new name of the theater with the tip of a wing, careful not to dislodge the letters spelling out the title of the upcoming production: *A Turtle in Love, Singing.*

The girl invited officers to stay for the rehearsal, which they did. Based on what they witnessed, Green Lake Police advises citizens to attend. It might just change your lives.

■

Tara Campbell is an award-winning writer, teacher, Kimbilio Fellow, fiction co-editor at Barrelhouse, *and graduate of American University's MFA in Creative Writing. Publication credits include* Masters Review, Wigleaf, Electric Literature, CRAFT Literary, Uncharted Magazine, Daily Science Fiction, Strange Horizons, *and* Escape Pod/Artemis Rising. *She's the author of the eco sci-fi novel* TreeVolution, *two hybrid collections of poetry and prose, and two short story collections from feminist sci-fi publisher Aqueduct Press. Her sixth book,* City of Dancing Gargoyles, *is forthcoming from Santa Fe Writers Project (SFWP) in fall 2024. She teaches creative writing at venues such as Johns Hopkins University, Clarion West, The Writer's Center, and Hugo House. Find her at www.taracampbell.com.*

SHEPHERD
NOT SHEEP

■

Simon Strantzas

Our tiny village, Drei Fluss, has three rivers and seven bridges. Under each bridge is a troll.

The trolls arrived the summer before last and no one in the village knows what to do about them so the council called a meeting. It's so well-attended people are jostling in the aisles. Everyone has an opinion about the trolls—why they moved in and why they won't leave.

Frau Knut sternly says they came because our new concrete bridges are more hospitable to them. But Herr Dirge asks then about Gusen Bridge, our wooden footbridge, and Frau Knut quietly sits down.

Her cousin, Frau Ulrich, snickers and says it has nothing to do with the bridges. It's the people. Trolls like being close to people for obvious reasons. She doesn't say what those reasons are, but I think I can guess.

And Herr Buag? He trembles and says they're an act of God. A punishment for our heathen ways. Only his son, Egon, applauds. The rest, judging by their reaction, don't know what the word "heathen" means.

Councillor Holler, a small, nervous man, bangs his tiny gavel. The reason the trolls are here doesn't matter. They're here, so what are we going to do about it?

Herr Oskar, our shopkeeper, has a suggestion: why don't we hire someone to kill them? Everyone nods or claps when he says this, and his face fights off a wave of smugness. But Jutta doesn't nod or clap. That's because Jutta believes there aren't any trolls in Drei Fluss, and there never have been.

She whispers to me that this lie about trolls infuriates her. She says the Council wants to scare us because it makes it easier for them to control us.

I whisper back and ask what it is, exactly, that they want to make us do. I try to sound curious, but it's hard when inside I'm pleading she'll just go back to how she was before.

She says they want Drei Fluss to become a tourist village. Tourist villages are rich villages, and the best way to become one is to be interesting. A village with seven bridges sounds quaint and boring. A village with make-believe trolls under those seven bridges doesn't. It doesn't sound safe, no matter how safe it actually is. She says that's what makes it interesting.

I ask her if she thinks Drei Fluss is safe in the same whisper, but I'm straining against my agitation. I can't understand what's happened to her. I'm not even sure it's still Jutta. Maybe the trolls got to her. Maybe they replaced her. Can trolls do that?

She smiles. It's the kind of smile that barely curls her lips; instead, it rolls them back over her teeth like a window blind. I don't like it. I'm about to tell her how unsafe Drei Fluss really is, but Councillor Holler does it for me by summoning Frau Miran to the front of the room.

She steps to the front of the room carrying a photograph of her missing daughter, Fiona. We all knew Fiona, and we've all seen the photograph—it's been in the local newspaper every week, plastered to every posterboard throughout Drei Fluss. We all know something happened to her, which is why it's so hard to look at Frau Miran. But she looks at every one of us. Up there, from the lectern, she stares with a scorching anger. I want to believe that's all it takes to prove the trolls to Jutta, but she's unmoved. Worse than break my heart, it disappoints me.

Frau Miran's voice cracks as she starts speaking. That crack never really goes away.

You all know what happened to my Fiona, her mother says with a timbre so sharp I feel its cut. It was those trolls. Those vile, putrid trolls. They took my little Fiona and that was it. We never found her afterward. Never found even a trace of her. My Fiona was only twelve years old and had barely started life. Did you know she spoke to fairies? She liked to go out in thunderstorms because that's when they heard her best. She loved bad weather outside more than she loved the inside. She was strange and darling and I never wanted to live without her. And now I have to. Because of those trolls. You know what they are, and you don't do anything about them. Even after what they did. To my poor Fiona ...

Her face contorts as she trails off, the lines of her face becoming a scribble. Jutta whispers out the side of her mouth, asking if Frau Miran is about to cry. But she doesn't and Jutta scoffs. You don't believe this, do you? she asks me. So I ask her back, a bit too loud, what *she* thinks happened to Fiona. Jutta shrugs, doesn't know; she isn't Fiona's mother. Frau Miran must hear us because her face turns a color that doesn't look good or right on a person.

Before she can speak, Councillor Holler rushes to applaud. The rest of us follow. Even Jutta claps but I can tell it's insincere. Frau Miran's grimace is wounded as she glances at us while stepping from the front of the room. Jutta continues clapping. She doesn't care if she's the last one making noise.

Jutta and I met in the before-times, when Drei Fluss was troll-free and all the bridges were wooden and boring. I went to Hiachst Park, just on the other side of Schwecat Bridge, because I'd run out of places to hide at home, and because there was nobody around who wanted to seek. I found Jutta seated on the swings, wearing a pair of heavy black shoes and a dirty dress whose latticed hem was torn above the knee. She rested as limp as a rag doll against the chains as she swayed. I stood back on the edge of grass, not knowing what to do. After a moment she seemed to come alive, bolting upright, and the way she looked at me ... I knew right then she didn't need to speak because I could see my thoughts on her face. I walked over and announced my name was Maud, then gave her my strongest push. She screamed with delight as her feet left the ground. From that moment, we were inseparable, and I never had to worry about being alone again.

But the trolls changed everything. That Jutta is gone now. This Jutta wouldn't be delighted. She'd narrow her eyes and ask why I was at Hiachst Park and what I wanted with her. This Jutta wouldn't let me anywhere near her, or if she did, she'd test me first to be sure I was real. She would never try to make me feel welcome. She'd be just like everyone else—trying to make me believe I don't belong.

It would bother me except it doesn't matter anymore. No one goes to Hiachst Park now, anyway. Or any park. I definitely don't. Not since Fiona vanished. It ruined Frau Miran's life and it's ruined the lives of everyone in Drei Fluss, too. With the exception of maybe Jutta's.

The roads are empty when we walk home from the village meeting. Jutta is up on the curb, one foot in front of the other, bony arms outstretched like she's on the highwire. I don't look at her. I just want to be alone, but I'm also terrified she'll go. There's a troll nearby. I can smell it.

Not that I've ever seen one. Not really. I know other people say they have, but not me, though I've come close. Once, I glimpsed a shadow rise up from behind an old pushcart on the side of Lonnie Road, and my whole body froze up. But it wasn't because of the shadow. It was the smell. Trolls have a particular odor—like clothes that haven't been washed in a long time. Sour and greasy. It lingers in your head for so long you still smell it even after you shouldn't. I knew as soon as I smelled it what it was. And I ran home like I'd never run before.

Jutta hates this story. She asks me if I've ever smelled a river before, then reminds me we have three of them and they all smell bad. It's the algae and the scum. She says all I was smelling was river water and calls me stupid. Even though I know she's wrong, she's so certain that for a moment I doubt myself. Could she be right? Then Jutta opens her mouth and my questions vanish.

She tells me the village has got me so worked up over the troll conspiracies that I'll believe anything now. Then she laughs and asks in a snarky voice if I think the wind is caused by trolls breathing, and if I think it gets dark because the trolls switch the sun with the moon every night. Trolls are all anyone ever talks about, she says, and it's not funny anymore.

Jutta doesn't listen when I tell her for a fact what I overheard my mother discussing with her friends. The Bauer boy, Chime, had been on Fuscher Bridge and narrowly avoided being taken by the troll that lived under it. Chime said the thing had hands as big as his head, but the strangest thing was its eyes. My mother's friend asked what they looked like, but if there was an answer I couldn't overhear it, no matter how hard I pressed my ear to the wall. I still shivered, though. And I shiver now as I tell Jutta. She just snickers and picks up a rock from the ground to hurl as far as she can into Köhler River. It's a bunch of bullshit, she says. Chime is always making up stories. She asks if I remember when he pretended he didn't believe in ghosts until he was dared to go into the cellar of St. Alphege Church and the upperclassmen locked him in? They only held the door for five minutes, but Chime still wet himself. Jutta guffaws and picks up another rock to throw. I don't think it's as funny as she does, but I don't laugh as much as Jutta anyway.

Sometimes I wonder what my life would be like without her. What if tomorrow my parents sat me down and told me that it was Jutta that had gone missing; that everyone thought a troll had got her instead of Fiona. What would I feel? I don't think I'd be surprised. And I don't think I'd cry. I think I might be relieved. Just a little. But I don't know. Nobody knows how they'll feel before they feel it. The only thing I'm sure of is Fiona would not have sat with me at a council meeting about Jutta. Not that there would have been a meeting.

Jutta jumps down from the curb. As she lands on the cobblestones she wants to know, if nobody has ever seen a troll, how is everyone so sure they know what one looks like. And why am I so sure they're the ones telling the truth.

The smell, I start to say, but she interrupts me.

Not the smell again.

I tell her a good friend would believe me.

She tells me a good friend wouldn't believe such stupid things.

I pick up my stride to get ahead of her. But Jutta doesn't like being left behind, and she doesn't like it when I stop speaking to her, so she hurries to keep pace.

I'm sorry, Maud, she says. I don't acknowledge her. I don't slow down. I wait to see if she'll tell me why she's sorry, but she doesn't. We just walk in silence—me staring straight ahead, her staring at her feet. I don't know how long we go without speaking to each other, but it might be a record.

We need to cross Krottenback Bridge to get home, but Krottenback is probably the bridge I'm most afraid of. The other six bridges have trolls, everybody knows this, but Krottenback is our biggest bridge which means the biggest troll must live there. It smells nearly every time I run over it. I should run this time, too, but I know Jutta will refuse to follow and I don't want to run with her watching. I know I shouldn't be embarrassed but I am.

Jutta must know this. She's probably counting on it.

Jutta nods at the bridge and says: Well, that's worrying, isn't it?

I ask her what she means.

She points as we get closer—not so close that something could snatch us, but not so far that something couldn't. I look and I see the bridge I've always seen. Then I see more.

It's crooked, she says. Twisted like cherry licorice.

It's not that bad, I tell myself. It's only just a hump midway across. The concrete is buckled, lowered on one side just enough to be noticeable. There's nothing interesting or unique about it.

But maybe that's why it bothers me. It's the mundanity. After so long living with the fear of the trolls, of their mysterious habits and behaviors, something as ordinary as twisted concrete fills me with a kind of unshakeable dread. Or maybe it's the flavor of the air that has changed. It's become sour and just a little bitter. As I notice this, I also notice one other thing: it's become quiet. I can't hear anything, not even my own breathing.

I don't like this, I say. Something isn't right.

Jutta sniffs the air. Laughs in a way that doesn't reassure me.

I suggest we take the long way home tonight.

The two of us retreat from Krottenback Bridge, back down Wassa Road, past Monad's Butchers. We turn the corner at Perrera Lane and sneak through a few back alleys as a shortcut until we find ourselves at Piesting Bridge. This bridge is flat, and we can hear the crickets along the riverbanks which I think means it's safe. As a precaution, though, I remove my shoes and walk across the bridge barefoot. I hope my feet are as quiet under the bridge as they are on top of it. About halfway across Jutta shouts: Hey! Do you hear snoring? and I'm suddenly running so fast my bare feet go numb. I don't hear Jutta's cackles until I'm already bent over and panting on the other side.

It's an hour later than usual when I reach my house but at least I reach it. My mother's face is white as a paper when she sees me, her eyes glossy and bloodshot. She hugs me so hard I worry she'll split me like a ball of dough. My father doesn't say a thing, but he looks relieved. They don't ask how the meeting went. And the next morning is the same as any other morning.

But it doesn't stay that way.

Herr Buag knocks erratically at our door during breakfast. My father makes a noise with his nose and wipes his mouth before standing. My mother's eyes stay glued to her porridge. Her spoon trembles. I can't hear what Herr Buag is saying but I hear enough to know it's a prayer. And I only hear that because my father prays with him.

Egon Buag is missing, I tell Jutta, later, while we sift through gravel along the edge of the road. I tell her everything I know: that after the village meeting they think Egon crossed over Krottenback Bridge to get home. A torn sleeve from his jacket was found on the Vakea Road side.

Did he run away with Fiona? she asks.

Of course not!

I never liked Egon. He was never nice to us.

Jutta!

I suppose you're going to tell me a troll took him.

How can Jutta say this? Egon's gone, I repeat. He's missing. He's probably dead.

Maud, don't be the sheep; be the shepherd.

What does that even mean?

It means you're choosing to believe these stories. Open your eyes.

I can't hide my irritation anymore. Jutta smiles.

Egon's body is found a few days later. Or, at least, parts of his body are found. Three of his limbs are found in a pile near Fischa Bridge. This surprises everyone as we all considered it the safest bridge. Egon's torso, though, is over by Krottenback Bridge, and when I tell Jutta she shakes her head with disgust. What I overheard from my father was it looked the way an animal does after a pack of wild dogs gets at it. The ribs were cracked open and there were ropes of intestines spread through the rushes alongside Miran River. I once got an accidental glimpse behind the curtain of Monad's Butchers and I still have nightmares about it. I can see it like a ghost in the room with me. I can't imagine how much worse Egon's remains must have been.

Jutta tells me she heard his liver was gone. She's probably trying to make me sick for fun.

I ask why his liver.

She shakes her head. Tells me the liver is the best part of the body. It's filled with all the delicious fats. It's like eating a stick of butter. If you're only going to eat one part of something, she tells me, it's the liver, hands down.

I didn't know that.

Her laugh is more like a derisive snort. Of course you don't, she says. Nobody wants us to know. Believe me.

Jutta sweeps up a rock and holds it out for me to inspect. It's a good one; a little green, but also gold, too, and the striations are all even. It could probably knock someone down if you hit them with it right, and I bet it could do almost the same to a troll. I'm mad she found it, to be honest, but I keep that to myself. Just because I don't think she deserves it doesn't mean she doesn't. What I believe and what's the truth are two different things. It's something I'm working on remembering because Jutta won't.

After the discovery of Egon, an emergency Council meeting is called. There's a different feeling in the air. As though all the anger of the village has finally metastasized, and real change is coming. We all feel it: Egon Blevin's death has catalyzed us into finally doing something.

Herr Oskar can't help himself. He reminds everyone that he had first suggested hunting the trolls down after Fiona disappeared. If we had, he says, Egon might still be alive. Frau Buag immediately sobs and the look Herr Oskar gives her gets imprinted on my mind. It's terrible. And makes me feel bad even though I didn't say a word.

Frau Knut asks if something so violent is necessary and it seems to split the crowd in half. After an hour a compromise is reached: the men of the town will try to secure the bridges and only if the trolls return will they try something more drastic.

They turn proudly to Frau Miran, but she surprises them with her hesitance. Even Jutta can't believe it. They ask does she not want to find the troll that ate Fiona and Frau Miran's face turns a color I've never seen before. She lowers her head as though she's embarrassed. Or maybe she's holding something back. When she looks up again, I don't understand the expression on her face but it makes me sad.

I don't know, she finally says, and if there's not a gasp my mind inserts one.

How can you say that? Councillor Holler asks.

Frau Miran seems lost to me. She admits she doesn't know what happened to Fiona, but that none of us do. No one has shown her a single piece evidence that a troll took her daughter. With the Buag boy there were at least remains and blood. There was something that said maybe a troll ate him—though even that isn't for certain. But Fiona? Her sweet Fiona? She's seen nothing. And if Fiona wasn't eaten by a troll, then maybe Egon wasn't either? How do any of us know?

All the adults in the room talk hurriedly among themselves, one shouting over the other. All the while Frau Miran ducks her head and stares are her feet. I'm too stunned to say much, and even if I weren't I don't think I'd want to. Not after turning to look at Jutta's smug and elated expression. Told you, she mouths.

Councillor Holler bangs his gavel and wrestles the crowd eventually. Frau Miran has not moved. When people calm enough for him to be heard he reminds us all—reluctantly, I think—that Frau Miran is grieving and we have to give her space. She isn't thinking right. But he also says we cannot wait on dealing with the trolls once and for all. If not for Egon and Fiona, then for all the other children who will most certainly follow. He says more but I can't concentrate over Jutta's muttered snickers. I try to remind myself the old Jutta must still be in there, somewhere. But it's increasingly harder to believe.

No one seems surprised to see the men on Krottenback Bridge early the next day. They have rope coils slung over their shoulders and tools hanging from their belts. Their faces are pale, which I know because Jutta says she saw them firsthand. She tells me she was on the bridge when they all marched across in a row. I want to know why she was there without me, and she says we don't need to be together all the time. She's never spoken to me like that before. She continues to describe what she saw: the way the men rappelled down ropes thrown over the side of the bridge; how some watched while the others worked. I ask her questions about what happened afterward, and she shrugs. It was a waste of time, she says, and there was no point to waiting around. Either the men declared they found no trolls after all, or they pretended they had because that's what the Council ordered.

When my parents think I'm asleep I overhear them discussing what happened afterward. Jutta was kind of right, I guess. The men admitted to not finding a troll under Krottenback Bridge. But they did find what a troll left behind. A hole, maybe ten feet tall, carved by hand into the rocky earth beneath the bridge and which went further into the darkness than any of them could throw a lit torch. They said the air spilling out of the hole smelled worse than the air above it, and three of the men had their legs turn wobbly before it occurred to any of them to cover their faces. I can suddenly smell it myself, even though we're nowhere near a bridge.

Something about the stench made the men angry enough to snap. My father whispers to my mother that he heard the men found a small table and chairs and smashed them, then made water over the debris before leaving so as to send a message. My mother is aghast, but my father's voice just gets this sound I've never heard before. It's hard and maybe distant. He says afterward that the men forgot who they were for a time and became animals. They tried to destroy everything they saw that might belong to the troll, and when they were done, they gathered up their equipment and went to the next bridge to do the same. Then, the next. They continued until they visited all seven bridges over our three rivers and left a warning under each: no troll is safe. After that my father doesn't say much so I sneak back to bed and wonder if I can believe it's finally over.

The next day, school has been canceled since we're not allowed to go near any of the bridges. Jutta doesn't care what people say she's allowed to do, though. She does what she wants even when I tell her not to, so I'm not surprised when I find her standing outside my window. I go down to meet her before my parents notice.

I ask her what's wrong as I toe the dirt, looking for rocks. Any rock will do at this point. I just need something to focus on.

She brushes my question away.

That's not important, she says. What's important is why is the Council continuing to pretend. They say it's about Egon but it's not. They say it's about trolls but it's not. It's not even about Fiona because nothing happened to her. It's all lies. It's all bunk. They just want us to be afraid. Just watch: soon they'll tell us they *need to do more to protect us from the trolls* so our taxes will increase to pay for it. It's just like what happens in the cities, except it's harder to get away with it in the cities because the people there aren't all sheep.

I wonder if Jutta has any idea what she's talking about, or is she just parroting words to sound smart. Either way, she sounds dumb and it makes me angry. Egon died. Fiona, too, probably. And for Jutta to say these things, even if she really believes them, is dangerous. People will start to listen to her stories because they don't know what else to do. The lies become like those rubber life preservers on the side of the bridges, and people will hold onto them past the point of knowing better.

I realize right then that telling her she's wrong isn't enough. I need to prove it to her. Prove to her that Fiona is missing. Prove to her that Frau Miran doesn't know where she is. I bend down and pick up the rock my foot has uncovered, one that's just the right size for my pocket, which means it's just the right size for my hand. It's covered in crystals that reflect the sun like tiny diamonds. But in the centre of the rock there's a crack that runs deep. Maybe if I can show Jutta the truth, really show her, then I'll be able to put the same kind of crack in her disbelief. And maybe that crack will spread and the rock in her will collapse and behind it will be the Jutta I used to know. The one I'd met on those swings in Hiachst Park, the one who's been with me every day for as long as I can remember. I miss that Jutta so much it hurts to think about her. All I need is one crack, just one. Because maybe Jutta is *my* life preserver. And without her to hang onto, I'm going to drown.

I immediately regret us knocking on Frau Miran's door. I feel Jutta's breath on my neck, hear her trying to bury her smirk, and I resist turning around and leaving. But only because the door has already swung open and Frau Miran is standing there in her plain frock, swollen eyes circled red and purple. Her hair is tied on top of her head in a loose knot. She looks more haggard than I've seen anyone ever. I catch only a glimpse of the house behind her, but it's enough to tell me she's given up.

She doesn't say anything, and neither does Jutta behind me. I hate this—playing middle monkey—but that's the game with Jutta. I need to say something to Frau Miran since us being there was my idea, but the voice in my head stammers and everything is harder than it should be. It's like my thoughts don't want to sit still, and as I struggle, I feel Frau Miran's nervousness radiate.

I knot my fingers as I screw up my courage. When I open my mouth, though, only jumbled nonsense comes out. Frau Miran impatiently tells us she's busy, but I think she sounds more scared. Waves of something else wash over me, too— a cocktail of sorrow and despair.

Jutta says we should run. But a noise from inside the house stops me. It's like a small throaty cough, maybe. But I must be imagining it. It can't be real. None of this can be. I glance at Frau Miran and her eyes look as though they're on the verge of crying again. It must be awful to have us here, confronting her. Reminding her of Fiona.

And I'm ashamed of myself for letting Jutta manipulate me. I wish a troll would spring up and swallow me whole.

I give it a moment but no luck.

Then that cough again. Louder. And this time Frau Miran's head turns.

She's heard it, too.

Jutta tugs on the back of my coat. I don't look at her. I already know what she's going to say. But I don't want to believe it. Jutta doesn't hesitate. She screams out Fiona's name then bolts out from behind me and pushes past Frau Miran into the house. Without thinking, I sprint after her. Frau Miran is too startled to catch me in time.

The house is cluttered and in disarray. I trip over the boxes and dishes and garbage that blanket the floor in thick litter. I lose balance, stumble, and it's too late to right myself before I narrowly miss knocking Jutta down. Instead, I spin and tumble to the floor in the middle of the sitting room, my knees taking the worst of it. That skinning pain distracts me momentarily from who is standing before me. From who Jutta is staring at. I get to my feet but lose my voice.

It's the closest I've ever been to a troll. It's too big for the room, its head nearly brushing the ceiling, and it's dressed in a torn yellow-stained undershirt and a pair of long thermal pants. In its giant hand is a teacup, so dwarfed it might as well not be there at all. The troll looks at me with frog eyes, as pale and cloudy as chunks of ice. Its bulbous nose sniffs the air. As though it can smell me. Whereas all I smell is it. The stench is so bad my eyes cry.

I can explain, Frau Miran hurries. I don't want her to explain. There's nothing I want less than her explanation.

It ate Fiona! I can't believe I have to say it.

Frau Miran's face splits like an overripe red tomato and she sobs. No, he didn't, she pleads. He couldn't. He wouldn't.

We didn't eat the girl. Didn't happen, the troll wheezes, giant hand placing the teacup down on the table between us. It keeps looking at me with those frog eyes.

Jutta tells me to ask it what it's doing here then. So I do.

It licks its lips with a purple tongue. Frau Miran is a beautiful woman. Beautiful. Said she'd let us stay. We can't go back to Krottenback Bridge any more. They want to get rid of us. Can you believe it? So jealous.

Frau Miran whimpers. It's like the groan of something straining under too much weight.

I back up. Jutta is smugly muttering I told you sos. I feel so sick I can barely remain standing. My insides squirm over themselves.

Don't, Frau Miran blubbers. Don't hurt him.

Hurt *him*? I think

The troll scratches the inside of its thigh through its thermal pants. It pulls a twisted face as half its mouth lifts.

Your council doesn't like us. They keep making up things. All lies.

Lies?

They hate that we're too strong, too smart. So they have to lie. Don't listen to them. Think for yourself.

But … Egon …

Did *you* see anything? No. Didn't happen. Why would we eat him? Not true. False information.

They *found* him, I say. Found what was left of him.

We know what they found. Wasn't that bad, actually. He wasn't completely eaten. Still mostly there. Anyway, wasn't us. We heard some people say the councillors killed Egon. We don't know if it's true. But someone should ask them. It would be interesting to know if they tell the truth. Not that it's a big deal, even if someone did eat him a little.

The crashing noise makes Jutta and me leap and scream. But it's not the troll. It's Frau Miran. She's collapsed to her knees. Wheezing, sobbing. Muttering. See? It's not him, she says. It's not. Fiona must still be alive.

Sure she is, the troll says. We're going to help find her. Troll's promise.

It puts an enormous finger aside its nose and taps.

I don't know who's worse: Frau Miran for believing the troll didn't eat Fiona, Jutta for still believing the troll isn't real, or the troll for believing I can't see through its lies. They're all too fogged up, unable or unwilling to see their truths.

Then I suddenly wonder if I'm the same. What do I believe that's not true? Thoughts race through my head too fast to litigate. I reach into my pocket and wrap my fingers around the rock Jutta and I found. It reassures and calms me. There's no way I'm as deluded.

You don't think? Jutta says, as though inside my mind.

I turn and look at her, surprised. She's standing a few feet away, arms crossed and smirking.

The troll picks up a pile of clothing from the floor. It's a number of shirts torn and stitched together into one larger shirt. The troll slips its arms into the half-made sleeves. Then helps Frau Miran to her feet.

I tell Jutta that none this makes sense, and she just nods her head like what I'm saying is obvious. Then she asks me why everything needs to make sense all the time.

Because, I tell her, it's the only way I know what's real.

This is when Jutta laughs, and it sounds like the world coming undone

What's real? she chuckles. Nothing is real but what

we've been told to believe. We spend our tiny lives in these tiny houses, and everyone says they'll only believe their own eyes. But they're all blind, so they listen to anyone who tells them something is there, even if it isn't. You tell me, how can anyone know what real even means anymore.

I feel something in the pit of my stomach. Like there's something important I should see but I can't. Jutta is grinning, but that grin is starting to falter. I squeeze the stone in my pocket harder than ever before. It feels like something is about to break. I look at the troll holding Frau Miran in its giant arms; but it's Jutta who's trembling.

You're lying, I finally say, but when I do the troll just looks at me queerly.

Who are you talking to? it asks.

But honestly, I don't even know anymore.

Simon Strantzas is the author of six collections of short fiction, including Only the Living Are Lost *(Hippocampus Press, 2023), and editor of several anthologies such as* Aickman's Heirs *(Undertow Publications, 2015). He is also co-founder and Associate Editor of the irregular non-fiction journal,* Thinking Horror, *and columnist for*

Weird Horror *magazine. Collectively, he's been a finalist for four Shirley Jackson Awards, two British Fantasy Awards, and the World Fantasy Award. His stories have been reprinted in* Best New Horror, The Best Horror of the Year, The Year's Best Weird Fiction *and* The Year's Best Dark Fantasy & Horror, *as well as published in* Nightmare, Cemetery Dance, Postscripts, The Dark, *and* elsewhere. He lives with his wife in Toronto, Canada.

VISIONARY

Sarah Starr Murphy

It is the dead hot held breath before a summer storm, and the pit of my stomach clenches in anticipation. Today is the summer solstice, and the world feels bleached from the strength of the sun. At the stove, I have a small pot of water about to boil. I watch as it does, burbling and bubbling. The water flings itself up and out of the pot, splattering onto the stove. I take a step back to protect my bare toes.

Another contraction starts to swell, the feeling a buzzing deepening twisting in my core, and I grab the edge of the counter, bend and moan. As it recedes, I gasp a breath.

There is an egg in the water, bobbling violently. It cracks against the side and releases a thin stream of white, cooking instantly in the water, clouding over. The water is boiling far too hard, but I do not reach to turn it down.

They said they could fix the way my husband's face blurred in the center. The doctor checked my eyes, gave me new glasses. When I looked with those new lenses, my husband was crisp, his features and jawline distinct. See, they said. See.

Every morning lying in bed, before I put my glasses on, Ethan's face is fuzzy. Nothing else in the room, just his face. I thought the problem was only with him, but then one day I answered the door without my glasses. The mailman's face was a soft pink smear under his curly red hair. After I closed the door, I turned on the television, flipped through channels. Every man's face a smudge.

Ethan tells me, stop misplacing your new glasses. We found the solution; it fixes the problem. Wear the damn glasses.

. . .

It's logical, so logical, and so I do.

One night, in bed with my new glasses dutifully in place, I notice that Ethan's hand on my stomach takes up more space than it did before. With the heel of his palm resting in the curls of my pubic hair, his fingers usually landed a few inches above my belly button. But his palm is there, and his fingers are rolling my nipple between them. His hand covers my entire torso, and the realization makes me catch my breath. Ethan takes this for desire and presses his lips to mine. The frame of my glasses presses into the soft flesh of my face.

The ophthalmologist promises the newest prescription will fix both the blurry faces and this new large-handed problem. And they do. The doctor's hands, which moments before had been catcher's mitts, shrink down to normal when I put on the glasses. Small, delicate hands he has, actually.

. . .

Ethan worries, of course, about my problems with my eyes. He makes pronouncements about cataract surgery, and although he knows nothing about it, he means well. I know he does. He's a man who came to me in a dream, before I saw him standing at the end of a lonesome dock in Maine, one late August day when the sky refused to warm and the fog was suffocating. I couldn't see the dock, but I knew he was there, because I'd seen him in my dream. I walked to the end of the dock and there he was, the man who would become my husband. We talked about the fog, the way it distorted the beam of the lighthouse across the water, the way it conjured the warbling of the loons. When I turned to leave, Ethan handed me a tin bucket of mussels he had plucked himself from the rocks, packed in eelgrass and topped with a splash of frigid water. His hand touched mine, and we both smiled.

Now we live far from the ocean, and maybe that is the problem. Maybe my eyes cannot adjust to the ceaseless still of the prairie. Landsick, perhaps. When I stand on our front porch, I look out over vast plains of prairie, the grasses and flowers waving in the summer heat. People say they resemble the ocean, but those people cannot have an intimate knowledge of the ocean. They have not felt the salt hardening into crystals on their skin, or the rush of saltwater into their ears. The prairie grasses are a vision unto themselves; they are not the ocean. There is so much flat land, so much arid sky. Perhaps the dryness is warping my vision, wrinkling the edges of my eyeballs like a raisin.

I call my parents and they are worried. My mother says intraocular cancer killed her great-aunt. My father wants to know if I am experiencing migraines to go along with my aura, visual ephemera, hallucinations, visions. I say no, but they do not believe me. They tell me to listen carefully to the ophthalmologist and do exactly as he says. They want me to get contacts I can wear all night long, worried about me waking and seeing such things.

My older sister, when my parents call her and she calls me, is full of answers. Perhaps I have synesthesia. Perhaps I am experiencing an allergy attack or a mild stroke. Perhaps I am dehydrated. Perhaps I am developing psychic vision. Mara warms to this last possibility, asks if I've ever noticed cold pockets of air in the house, if I've ever felt like I wasn't alone.

· · ·

I hang up with Mara and go outside so that I can breathe. I sit on the front steps, watch the grass for movement. There are small creatures called thirteen-lined ground squirrels living in my lawn. Halfway between a chipmunk and a squirrel, they have stripes down their backs and build burrows underground like prairie dogs. My neighbor, who asked that I call her Miss Bea, tells me that I should have my husband take a look at them before they become a real nuisance.

"They'll destroy your whole lawn, then head over here for mine," she says. I nod, but I won't bring it up with Ethan. I love to watch the curious faces poking up out of the holes in my otherwise bland lawn. They scurry from hole to hole, fat bellies swaying from side to side, their striped backs shining in the bright prairie sun. They are never out of focus or the wrong size, even early in the morning when I forget my glasses.

I come home from the store one day to find Ethan cleaning out our bedroom. It's true, we've accumulated a lot of things we don't need. I look into the black garbage bag sagging on the bed.

"My old glasses!" I reach for them, but Ethan takes two quick steps across the room, puts his hands gently on mine.

"You don't need them, darling. You can't see a thing with them. You have the new ones."

He smiles, and I wonder when his teeth have gone so terrifying, each of them coming to a sharp point, a jagged mouthful of fangs. He sees the fear in my eyes.

"What? What is it?"

"I liked my old glasses," I mumble.

"That's not it," he says, leaning in, pressing my new glasses further up my nose with one finger. "What is it now? What do you see?"

He moves closer and closer and I fear he will bite so I say, "Your teeth, your teeth."

My third prescription in as many weeks fixes the fang problem as well as the blurring and the big-hands. Ethan kisses me and I can feel, my tongue in his mouth, that his teeth are flat and perfectly normal. I am afraid of what will happen if I kiss him without my new glasses, so I start to wear them all the time. We often have sex in the middle of the night, hands straying and bodies following before we are fully awake, so I start sleeping with my glasses on. What if he sank his teeth into my shoulder and came away with a mouthful of flesh?

The next morning, I watch the ground squirrels skitter from hole to hole, a mother followed by babies. Pups, I think. I press a hand to my warm, round stomach. I hope the baby will be well. My obstetrician says it's possible that my visual artifacts, his term, are a result of elevated hormones.

"Make women a bit crazy," he says, with a jovial laugh. "Like everything else, it'll be better once you deliver."

I do not say anything about the fact that his Adam's apple has protruded so far that it has become like a marlinspike. I had a marlinspike once, on my sailing knife, a long, pointy piece of metal used for loosening tight knots. Cone-shaped, slightly curved. I loved the feel of it in my fingers, the way it eased into a knot and broke it open. The violation.

I try not to tell Ethan about the fact that his Adam's apple has also transformed, but when he presses in to kiss me, eager to hear about the baby's measurements, his spike presses against my throat until I gasp and choke and then I must tell him. Grimly, he puts me in the car. He slams the door once I am inside, does not speak on the way to the ophthalmologist.

When we leave with a brand-new pair of glasses, he says, "I can't do this if you don't talk to me. We are a team. You need to tell me what's going on."

I nod, and agree, because what else.

"The obstetrician said maybe after I deliver."

Ethan nods but says nothing more. It starts to rain on the way home, and I worry about the ground squirrels, about their tunnels getting wet, their puppies cold. There is nothing I can do.

Miss Bea knocks on my screen door late in the afternoon, and I am afraid that she will yell at me again about the squirrels, but no, she is holding a cobbler.

"Peach," she says, "for good luck. My gram always said that peach in pregnancy makes for a round-cheeked baby." She stares at my stomach, and I look down, worried that it might have changed, but it is still a benign globe pushing out the front of my shirt and working my unbuttoned jeans slowly down off of my hips.

"Thanks," I say. I cannot imagine eating the cobbler, with the heartburn even now pressing its hot fingers on the back of my throat, but it is not nice to say so.

"I hear you puking, you know," she says. I don't know what to say to this, so we both watch as one of the ground squirrels pokes its head up from a hole nearby. It looks first at me, then at her, twitches its whiskers, and disappears.

"It'll all be over soon. Everything will be better once you've delivered."

"After the baby's born," I say.

"Yes. It's a miracle, how fast you feel better. After."

I nod, but she is looking at where the ground squirrel has disappeared and I think she will say something else, something about poison or traps or exterminators, but she sneezes.

"Bless you," I say.

She looks hard at me and says, "You too, my child." She walks away and I wonder if she, Miss Bea, is secretly holy. When she gets to her door and has forgotten all about me, she reaches a hand back to pluck a wedgie from her voluminous skirt and I think, probably not.

• • •

"Visions," my sister Mara insists, when she calls me late at night. She calls every night now, worry threading her voice. I take the call down in the kitchen so as not to disturb Ethan.

"You are seeing behind the veil," Mara says. I take a box of sea salt from the cabinet and pour a small amount in my cupped hand. I stick the tip of my tongue into the pile of flakes as she speaks, try to remember the dark, briny suck of the tide.

"I'm going to send you crystals," she says, "to keep you safe until I can get there." I say nothing because I know there is no stopping her.

They come express, dozens of small sparks of color jumbled in a box, and I run my fingers through them: amethyst, quartz, garnet, and jasper. Most of them are the size of a piece of gravel and about as attractive, unpolished. I pull my hand out and see that it's bleeding; I have cut a finger on a sharp edge of crystal. I pick up the one polished stone, a pretty thing of blue, purple, and green. Labradorite, says Mara's note, for power and protection. I slip the labradorite into my pocket, but I start to wonder if my big sister has lost her mind.

I bring the box outside and scatter the small crystals like seeds over the green of the lawn. I sit on the stoop until a ground squirrel comes investigating, whiskers twitching. She looks me in the eye, this mama squirrel, and then tucks a chunk of amethyst into her cheek, darting away with it to her burrow. I wait but she does not return. That night, waiting to sleep, I imagine a sparkling cache hidden under the grass, the pups tumbling around in the refracted light. The labradorite is warm in my fist.

Ethan is out when my labor starts, completing a songbird survey in the wide-open prairie, counting aggressive redwing blackbirds and dainty, razor-billed kestrels. I could call him, but I don't. First labors always take ages, everyone has assured me. I fill a pot of water and put it on to boil, thinking, a solstice baby. I will make an egg, for strength, for luck. I've been told that once I enter the hospital, I won't be allowed to eat until after the baby comes. I am hungry.

The egg jumps in the water and I fish it out with a spoon. Slowly, I peel away the jagged shell, press the rubbery flesh into the salt cellar before taking a bite. I eat between contractions, thinking of the ocean. When I am finished, I call my husband. He comes fast, packages me into the car and we drive away. The morning sunshine has vanished, clouds are dark and low; it begins to rain. Every bump in the road is excruciating, my contractions close together, and then there is a hard thud.

"What was that?" I ask, wincing.

"Nothing, pothole," he mutters, but he looks shiftily in the rearview mirror. I look over at him, and I know that it was the mama ground squirrel.

"Nothing?" I ask.

"Nothing," he says, "concentrate on breathing, baby."

A wave of pain hits and I double over in the seat, panting. I have forgotten the labradorite on the kitchen counter, but it is much too late now.

They rush me to a delivery room, I am so obviously in transition when I arrive, and the nurse gets me settled into the bed, hikes my knees up to my ears. I had always imagined birthing as something that happened far away from the me that lives in my brain, far down at the other end of my body, somewhere around my toes. All hunched up like this I find I am uncomfortably close to my own vagina and wish I was further away. The pain is indescribable and everywhere, and I am well past the opportunity for an epidural. My husband is by my side, holding my hand.

"You're doing great, babe," he says. I glance over at him and his face is blurred. I press my newest glasses up my nose with a finger, but it doesn't help.

I'm hit by a fast contraction, then another.

"Time to push, hon," says the nurse, cheerfully, like she's announcing good news.

I bear down.

"Yes, that's it, good! Good girl."

I look at my husband, panting with effort. He glances down then away.

I feel the nurse cleaning something up.

"Just blood," says the nurse, smiling blandly. Another contraction and another push. I can hear the nurse calling urgently into the little communication device attached to her scrubs. My doctor walks in.

"Well, here we go! Say goodbye to your modesty, hon, we're going to have a baby!" His face is so smudged it is almost erased. The glasses are no longer working.

Another contraction tears through me and I scream and push like an animal.

"Gentle, now, little pushes," he says, sliding down between my legs and putting his hands everywhere. I close my eyes to block him out and do what my body requires. Excruciating, blinding pain, and then the head is out. Another push and I can feel the whole baby born.

Everyone is cheering and yelling but I am afraid to look.

"Open your eyes now, mommy, let us know you're okay," says the nurse, slipping back up beside me. I focus on her face. I press my glasses so far up my nose they bite into my skin. She has blue eyes, thin lashes globbed with mascara, and a poppy seed stuck in her front teeth, but her smile is genuine. "Here you go, darling," she says, and puts the baby on my chest.

I look down and she says, "A boy."

But I know. I know from his pointed teeth, his oversized hands, his blurry face, his sharp little Adam's apple. He begins clawing his way toward my face. In a panic I look up, and my husband and the doctor are the same. They grin at me with their terrifying teeth and I begin to scream.

They don't take the baby right away. The kind nurse picks him up and brings him to the other side of the room. Ethan looks so embarrassed by my outburst that I stop screaming. My stomach contracts as if in response to the silence.

"Placenta!" announces the doctor, hoisting the bloody mass in the air.

"Mara," I say, "I want my sister."

"Oh, there's plenty of time for all that later," the doctor says. "We don't want to overwhelm you."

Ethan nods, strokes my hand. I try so hard to focus on his blurry face.

"Just going to stitch you up," the doctor says, "We've got quite a tear on our hands!"

He is so close, tugging and prodding, that I can smell the onion on his breath.

The room is dry, cold, and sterile. I tip my head to try to get a glimpse of sky out the window. I can see only the brick wall of another hospital wing.

There is a knock on the door.

"Come on in!" the doctor shouts, and I see a dozen young men in white coats dart inside.

"Ah, rounds!" The doctor pats my bare thigh with his bloody, gloved hand. "You, my dear, are fortunate to be in the state's premiere teaching hospital. Don't be shy boys, come on over. I'm just stitching – see how she's torn almost to the anus? Impressive, isn't it?"

Their teeth are so sharp, their hands are so big. Their Adam's apples spike below their blurred faces. They lean in, staring.

There is another knock on the door. One of the residents answers and I can hear Mara's voice.

"I'm her sister. Let me in."

"I'm sorry," the resident says, "She's in no fit state for company at the moment."

"Mara!" I yell, but Ethan shushes me, frowning, and a resident shuts the door. I know then that Mara is much too late.

"How many fingers?" asks the doctor. He holds up one hand, still gloved and covered in my blood.

I know I should say five, but there are eight, spiraling out from the palm like a starfish. Eight. I take off my glasses, but the number doesn't change. I let the glasses clatter to the floor, unnoticed.

"How many?" he asks, his voice singsong. He doesn't need me to answer; maybe he can read it in my eyes.

"Nurse!" he calls, and the woman reappears, the baby in her arms. The baby is wrapped in a thin blue blanket, but he is looking at me. His eyes are deep blue and there is a wisp of dark hair on the crown of his perfectly round head. He opens his mouth in a yawn and I see there are no sharp teeth, no teeth at all in his pink gums. His cheeks are full, his nose a snub of a thing, and his whole face is utterly in focus.

"Wait," I say, but the doctor speaks over me.

"It appears there are complications," the doctor says. "Sometimes this happens, after the birth." I feel Ethan's hand wrap around my forearm, his eight fingers strong.

The nurse does not look at me as she takes the baby away. I struggle to get up, but I cannot move my legs.

I am alone as the men turn their gazes on me, sharp as crystal.

"Don't worry," Ethan says, "We're going to get you the help you need."

■

Sarah Starr Murphy's writing has appeared or is forthcoming in The Threepenny Review, Epiphany, Nat. Brut, *and elsewhere. She's managing editor for* The Forge Literary Magazine *and eternally at work on a novel. She's a marathoner with dogs, kids, and epilepsy.*

THE SOUND OF SILENCE

Jennifer Lee Rossman

"I dreamt about it again," I tell the darkness, because I can't tell anyone else.

My words return to me, echoing softly so it sounds like there's another little girl down here in the old subway tunnels. Like I'm not the only one.

"The night they came down from the sky," I say, and pause to listen. I know there's nobody else, I know it's just me, but it almost feels like a conversation.

Wouldn't you know it, we had the same dream.

"When it was so bright, I thought it was daytime. And then the gods came down. And then everyone screamed, and then no one ever screamed again."

Mama used to scream a lot. Usually at me, usually for no reason I could do anything about. I don't miss that, but I do miss her voice.

My next words, I say real quiet on account of how I don't want to hear them echo. If I don't hear them, maybe they aren't true.

"I don't remember her voice."

Sometimes I think I do, but I only remember her talking about Honey Nut Cheerios being a good part of a balanced breakfast, so I think I must be remembering a lady from a commercial. I remember the words she would scream, the fear and shame I would feel, but not the way it sounded.

The other girl in the tunnels is crying. I wipe my eyes and stand up, following my narrow flashlight beam and using indecipherable graffiti as landmarks until I reach my favorite part of the subway.

The graffiti here doesn't look like words. It's ... something else, horizontal lines with circles on them. I still don't know what it means, but it's not words I would be able to read if there was anyone left to teach me.

Here, at this very spot, the echoes are magic. They take my voice and split it into infinity, sending it down multiple tunnels and bringing it back at slightly different times and with slightly different volumes so it sounds like there's dozens of people down here with me.

"You're okay!" I shout, as loud as I can, and then I listen, and try to believe what I hear.

• • •

Mama's mad when I come home, but then she's always mad at me for something.

This is a new kind of mad she didn't have before the gods came down. Back then, she mostly just had *Why can't you just be normal* and *You're being difficult on purpose*, but now she has *You have a secret.*

People don't have secrets anymore, not with everyone communicating telepathically, and she hates that she doesn't know where I go during the day. Even more than she hates me being different, and more than she hates hiding it from the gods.

She doesn't make a sound, but her mouth is a tight line and her eyes are screaming at me. Her eyes, and everything else about her. The energy in the house is made of screams.

People think autistic folks can't read other people's emotions. I don't know about anyone else, but I can. I just don't know what to do with the information, because I've known my mama all nine years of my life and I've never been able to figure out why I make her mad or how to make it better.

I stand there for a minute, like I'm waiting for her to ask where I've been, then I go past her into the kitchen. Every sound seems louder than it used to without the constant background chatter of TV or radio, every footstep and horrible scrape of chair leg against linoleum, and I wonder if I will ever get used to the way things are now.

It would help if I could hum, drown out some of the silence buzzing in my ears. I miss music.

I settle for tapping my fingernails on the side of the bowl as I pour and sort my cereal.

Mama's eyes are even louder now. Is it my tapping, or is it that I can't eat marshmallows in the same bite as the cereal like everyone else?

I wish I could say it doesn't bother me, that I can look down at my bowl and ignore the look on her face and pretend she isn't silently screaming at me about how much she wants to give me to them and let them fix me, but it does. It makes my stomach twist and my brain want to run and hide even though I feel like I can't move, and I'm not hungry anymore.

When I go to stand up, to make a quick escape and go burrow under a heavy blanket for a while, my hand hits the spoon. It falls to the floor with a clatter, and instinctively, I look at Mama.

I'm not psychic like everyone else, but I don't need to be. Her face is saying all the things her mouth used to.

How many times do I need to tell you to be more careful? You never learn. I don't think you're even trying. I think you're doing this on purpose. You like making my life difficult.

It's not a decision I make, I'm not even aware I'm doing it. I just go into survival mode, and it slips out.

"I'm sorry."

For a moment, it feels like the world has stopped again, my words echoing like infinity in my ears. I can't take the silence. Please, why won't she just scream at me. Just scream like she used to and everything will be back to like it was before.

But she won't. It's hard enough for her to hide thoughts about me talking; in a world full of mind readers, everyone would know if she screamed at me, and then they would do to her whatever it is they will do to me if they find out.

And it would be my fault.

That's why I run.

I have the dream again, just like most nights. It isn't a nightmare, it doesn't need to be. It's just memories. Those are scary enough on their own.

It was me and Mama. I can't remember where we were going, but it was important to her and she was mad at me for not wanting to wear a coat even though it wasn't that cold and the bulky collar made my soul itchy.

We walked down Main Street just as the streetlights were coming on, and I squinted at them to make their halos stretch and deform. That annoyed Mama, just like my tippytoeing on the cobblestone sidewalk to make sure I didn't touch the cracks, and just like my humming.

Busy evening. Lots of other people standing under the overhangs of stores and restaurants, talking without really saying much and somehow saying much more than they actually said. Other people always had secret nonverbal languages I couldn't speak no matter how hard I tried, no matter how mad Mama got at me for not trying hard enough.

I don't know what made her yell at me, what the last little thing was that made it into a big thing. All of a sudden she was grabbing my arm and screaming my name, and that's when it happened, when I was looking up at her furious face and the sky split open behind her, so loud I didn't even hear her anymore.

I never heard her again, her or anyone besides myself and my echoes. Because when the sky opened, everyone—except for me, I guess—met the gods and got the gift to communicate without talking, to look at someone and instantly share each other's thoughts.

At least, that's my best guess at what happened. No one has told me. No one would dare tell me, not out loud.

The dream always ends the same way, with them realizing it didn't work on me, and me screaming as they drag me away. And then silence as they make me just like them.

• • •

This is the first time I've woken up in the tunnels since that first night when I ran and ran without knowing where I was going.

It's quiet, like home, like the rest of the world, but even in the darkness that surrounds me like a blanket fort, I can feel the difference. This silence isn't afraid, it isn't curled up into a tight ball made of anxiety. This silence is peaceful, breathing with me, big and welcoming and full of possibility.

I let it sleep, wordlessly turning on my flashlight and letting the beam play on the colorful airbrushed words scrawled on the walls. I pretend that one is my name, the blue and purple one with the zigzag line underneath. Probably isn't, but until I figure out how to teach myself to read or find someone who isn't afraid to talk who can teach me, it still might be.

Maybe the gods can only communicate telepathically, maybe they're afraid of people they don't understand and that's why they tried to make us just like them. Maybe that's why Mama is so scared of people finding out I'm different, because they made people scared of people who are different. Because we can talk about them, we can make plans against them, and they would have no idea.

"But I'm just one person," I say, and my echo agrees.

• • •

Maybe I won't go back this time. Maybe I'll just stay here in the tunnels, talking to myself and pretending I know how to read the graffiti. Mama loves me, in her own not-loving way, but I'm not sure she'll miss me.

"I won't miss her," I tell the darkness. "Not any more than I already do. She's not my Mama, not ever since that night."

My Mama got mad at me a lot, but she told me bedtime stories. She talked to me. We sang together at the piano, and she tried to teach me how to turn the nonsensical lines and dots on the paper into music, and—

Music.

The graffiti that isn't words! It's music! I'm sure it is, and maybe I can remember how to read it—

I'm not walking. I'm holding completely still. So why am I hearing footsteps?

I switch off my flashlight and make myself very small. I try not to make a sound, but my pounding heart is loud enough that I'm scared it will give me away.

Mama must have followed me. Once upon a time, when her voice wasn't just a memory about cereal, I might have thought she was coming to bring me home. Not anymore.

Maybe I got a little bit of the psychic gift, just enough to know they would try to fix me if they ever found out I couldn't read minds, but I know that's true. And I know that's why Mama is coming for me: she's not going to hide me anymore, she's going to give me to them.

The footsteps are louder. The tunnels twist and play with echoes, I know that more than anyone. There's no way to be sure where they are, or how many people are coming. But maybe I can use that. Maybe I can get to another exit and …

And what? Run forever? It'll be the same thing wherever I go, people made to be scared of me because I'm just one little girl who's different.

A quiet sob slips out, and even though I clap my hands over my mouth, it's too late. I hear the tiny echo from deep within the tunnels, and as scary as that is, it almost feels safe. Like I'm not alone, I'm not the only one who's different.

I wish that was true. Maybe, if there were a lot of people like me, it would seem normal, not something to be afraid of and fix. If there were a lot of us, we wouldn't go down without a fight.

In the tiniest voice, I whisper to the tunnels, "I have an idea, but I'm gonna need your help."

I want to be quiet. I want to hold my breath and hide and hope they don't find me, but I can't.

Their footsteps grow louder, faster. If I can hear them, they must be able to hear me, and I'm counting on that as I run through the dark maze I've memorized, making no attempt to hide the sound of my shoes slapping on the concrete.

My shadow flashes faintly ahead of me. They must be close, they must see me in their lights, but I can't hear them anymore over the sound of my heartbeat.

I stop running when I reach my favorite spot, and I don't even have to turn on my flashlight to see the graffiti that isn't words; the lights of everybody behind me turn the wall bright as day. For the first time, I can see the whole thing at once, every line and note. I can see how it fits together.

It is a song, I was right. And I might not remember everything Mama taught me about reading music, but I remember enough to recognize the song. Mama used to sing it to me sometimes, back when she wasn't scared to do that.

I squint as I turn to face the people with the lights so bright that I can't see anyone beyond them, and I hold up my hands in a gesture that I hope means "wait a second before you take me."

I wish I could talk to them first, tell them how it feels to be hated and feared for something I can't change, something I wouldn't change if I could. That being different is only bad because of how people treat me, and that not being psychic doesn't mean I'm broken any more than being autistic does, and the only thing stopping me from reaching my potential is them and their fears.

That, maybe, there are other people like me hiding in the darkness, and we don't want to hide anymore.

But I can't say anything, because the echoes would give away the magic. So I guess I need to hope that they hear my unspoken words.

So I sing.

I sing, and my voice is shaky and weak like my courage. The lights are getting closer, hiding everyone's face, but I don't need to see them to know they want to yell at me just like Mama every time I slip up.

Then the echoes start finding their way back to us, each one a little early or late, some softer than others, a few distorted from bouncing through the tunnels until they sound like a completely different person. The lights stop coming toward me, some of them swing around like they're looking for the other people who dare communicate verbally.

I keep singing, and my voice is still shaky and weak, but you can't tell because it's not just one voice anymore, it's dozens, hundreds. Infinite. I am not the only one, and we won't be silent anymore.

Then there's another voice. Not one of my echoes, another, real person singing with me.

I remember that voice. And not from a Cheerios commercial.

Mama steps forward, becomes a silhouette and then a person. She reaches out, like to hug me, but remembers I don't like that and pulls away. Her echoes join mine first, and then the others, one by one by one.

This doesn't fix everything. Mama will still want to yell at me sometimes, I think that's just the way she is, and the gods will still be mad at people for talking. But it's something, it's a start, and maybe one day we'll live in a world where we sing instead of yelling.

For now, at least, I'm not the only voice in the tunnels anymore.

■

Jennifer Lee Rossman (they/them) is a queer, disabled, and autistic author and editor from the land of carousels and Rod Serling. They are one of the editors of Mighty: An Anthology Of Disabled Superheroes, *and their queer reincarnation thriller* Blue Incarnations *was published in January 2024. Find these books and read free stories on their website http://jenniferleerossman.blogspot.com and follow them on Twitter @JenLRossman*

THE LIGHTBULB CANNOT BE CHANGED

Sasha Brown

It was night in the tall city and the buildings stretched up to the clouds like highways. Windows like dotted yellow lines. Everyone was shuffling down the sidewalk at the same pace, hoodies up. I was too. I looked up, to see if I could see anything past the endless clouds.

You never could. The clouds never went away. No stars.

I tripped and stumbled into the guy ahead of me. Someone else knocked me down. Someone stepped on my foot.

A bony hand pulled me off to the side, under a little overhang in the concrete wall.

He was a skinny little guy, big ears, lank long hair plastered around his skull. "Caughtcha lookin up," he said. "I do it too."

"Oh." I turned to go.

"Wait. You wanna see stars?"

I backed away. "We're not allowed up there. The high floors aren't for us. They cut people for that."

"They just warn you the first time. And besides, they never catch anyone. You always do what you're supposed to?"

"Yeah. Why, don't you?"

He shrugged. "I have clinical optimism," he said, like he'd practiced this speech. "My brain got a chemical imbalance that makes it hard for me to see the world as it is. Like biologically speaking, I'm too happy. I take pills for it."

I looked around. People like that usually didn't say it out loud. It was embarrassing. "Why are you telling me?"

"Pick a hand." He held out two fists gleaming like maggots in the dark, knuckles up. I picked one; he opened it to show a little pill, gummy with sweat, stuck to the creases in his palm. He shook it off to the ground. "I don't take the pills no more. I just want to feel something, you know? You do too. I can tell."

I wasn't sure about that, but the thing was it felt like he was inviting me on an adventure. Out of all the people, this guy wanted to go somewhere with me. It would be nice just to make a permanent memory. Maybe I could borrow a little bit of whatever he had, or it would rub off on me. A little dangerous hope.

"How can you tell?"

He grinned at me with crooked teeth. "'Cause you picked a hand."

I didn't exactly smile back, but I went.

His name was Ray. We took the elevator up for a ways, but it stopped where you weren't allowed to go higher. The hallway was all cinderblocks and Ray went to a little door at the end. "They never lock it," he said. "They figure nobody's gonna try."

We had to trudge up five flights of stairs to the roof. Neither of us were used to exercise. I looked up at his flat ass while we climbed. There was a little smiley face drawn in magic marker on his saggy jeans.

"You promise no one will catch us?" I asked.

"No one ever checks."

"It's just that it's so bad if they do."

"They won't even cut you, the first time. First time is just a warning. It's your first time, right?"

He creaked one last door open, and we were out on the roof.

I peered over the railing. The clouds were sludge below us, and the buildings came up like shark teeth through gums.

"No, but look up," he said.

There were the stars.

Stars looked like you were in a basement with a bunch of other people and the lights were off and everyone was smoking cigarettes. It made me feel like I was at a party and we were going to take turns telling secrets.

Ray came over next to me and took my hand. It felt clammy but I let him do it.

"It's worth it, right?" he asked. He leaned his face up toward mine.

"Yeah." Our lips were so dry that it felt like any other body parts touching, like not a big deal, but his hand snaked between my legs and felt how excited I was, how badly I wanted to be here in this moment. I started to put my hand between his legs too, but he jerked away like he didn't want me to. I didn't push it. I barely cared, if I could just feel something. If I could just be under the cigarette stars with a boy's hand between my legs, both of us where no one was allowed.

I kept stealing glances at the stars, looking all around while we kissed, so I saw the shadows while he was still distracted. I heard the boots scraping on the concrete. I tried to push him away but he held on, like he didn't get it, while the gendarmes surrounded us.

They pulled us apart and Ray lost his shit, like a switch flipped, shrieking and struggling, eyes bulging. The gendarmes were all in black and they were waving flashlights all over the place. Through them walked a thin man in a white coat like a doctor. Flashlight beams zagged around, shining on his big round glasses.

"I'm so sorry to see you again, Ray," he said. Ray shut up when he saw him. The gendarmes aimed their flashlights at the doctor and he raised a black-gloved hand, Ray's slimy white pill glistening in his fingers.

Ray struggled, but it was no use. "Taylor didn't have nothing to do with this, Doc. It was me."

He turned to me then, his glasses like searchlights. "Taylor is your name? Poor child. So weak. Such a follower." He shook his head. "Happiness is a perverse thing. You've heard this before. It is a distorted view of the world, yes? Inaccurate."

The doctor held out his hand, and a gendarme brought a bulky briefcase to him. It clanked when he set it down. "The world is a dark place. It is not cruel to acknowledge this; it's cruel to deny it. Hope is a thing of cruelty."

"I wasn't going to have any hope," I said, my voice high with fear. "It was just my first time, I won't do it again." I kept looking at the briefcase. It had clanked like metal, like there was metal inside it. What was it? What metal things had he brought with him?

"A man reaches to change a burned-out lightbulb," said the doctor. "His ladder is unsteady. Everyone says, 'Watch out, you will fall!' But he does not listen. He keeps reaching until the ladder tips. There's a great clatter. Now everything is a mess, and still there is no light. What do we do with that man who cannot stop reaching to change the lightbulb?"

I cringed back as much as I could, but the gendarmes held me tight.

"We take his eyes from him, so he doesn't miss the light." The doctor looked only at me. "Or we take his hands, so he cannot reach for the bulb."

Ray screamed, arms pinned behind his back. "Do it to me!" he shrieked. "It's my fault!"

"But we have already taken so much from you." The doctor opened the bag. He brought out a scalpel in one hand. In the other, a cleaver. "Now, Taylor, your friend's trouble has spilled onto you, and you must choose. Eyes or hands."

I looked wide-eyed over at Ray. "Did they already catch you?" The gendarmes braced themselves to hold me up. "Did they already cut you?"

"I'll take the pills forever," Ray gurgled. "I swear, sir."

"I didn't even look up," I said. "He made me."

"What a difficult moment for you, Taylor." The doctor nodded his head, sympathetic. "What a position Ray's awful hope has put you in. Eyes or hands."

The worst thing is to be helpless while pain comes for you. To be warned. "Please," I begged. "I'll do anything."

"If you do not choose," he said, "we will take both."

I looked up at him, pleading, but his glasses masked his face.

"Eyes," I whispered.

He dropped the cleaver, stepped forward and jerked my head up by my hair, and the scalpel sank into my eye. I squeezed my eyelids shut as it went in, and it cut through them too. I drew in my breath like I'd stepped into icy water. I could feel the blade behind my eye, stabbing inside me. It wiggled back and forth as the gendarmes held me steady, rotating my eyeball in its socket before it flipped it out of me. With my one eye I saw the other impaled, a ruined thing.

He shook the scalpel irritably once, three times and it splatted on the ground. He bore my head back again. Gloved fingers forced my eyelids open. The cigarette stars watched me. The blade was slow this time; it tickled my eyelashes, dimpled my cornea. An unbearable blackening pressure came, and then my last eye popped and the windows closed on my mind and it was just helpless agony. I heard Ray howling somewhere, short and rhythmic exhalations, as though not so much a protest as a song.

One night I walked home in a light rain, so light I could hardly feel it, and I stopped in the middle of the sidewalk. The stream of people went on around me. Everything went around me now. Sometimes I would stop, force people to veer. Look at the power of my scarred and empty face. I could hear their footsteps falter as they avoided me.

I took my sunglasses off and turned my face toward the sky. I tried to remember the stars puffing like cigarettes. How it felt like I had been invited to a party. I let the rain spatter down, pooling in my eye sockets. It seeped into my sinuses, dripped out my nose.

The trudge of footsteps altered twice. Once for me, and then again a little ways away. I was a little hole in the noise of the busy sidewalk, and there was another hole. The other hole moved closer to me, and I couldn't hear the space but only the people moving around it, and then we were just one bigger silent spot. I knew it was him, but I didn't say anything. He didn't either. After a while I walked off and his silence receded and was gone.

I began to stop more and more. In the aisle at the grocery store, I would just stand there; people would have to back their shopping carts up. In line at the coffee shop, I would see how long people waited before stepping around me. No one said anything. No one jostled me or yelled.

Ray was often there. I could feel him. He never participated. His cart didn't join mine in the frozen food aisle. He was just there.

One day I walked into the street. The cars hissed to a stop as I went, a quiet pneumatic sound. Their passengers were silent. I felt the cars alert and heavy, waiting for me as I stood motionless in the intersection.

Everything was still and quiet. Everyone stopped for me. I wondered how long I could stand there before someone took me away.

I could hear Ray coming. He walked behind me, whispering as he passed: "Don't be an asshole. Meet me tonight."

After a while I walked out of the intersection; the cars hissed to life again and everything kept on going.

"They'll finish you if you keep doing shit like that," he said. "They'll cut until there's nothing left." His voice echoed around the brick walls. We were standing in a tunnel, like in a sewer or something. I hadn't wanted to follow him down at first, but no one else had even talked to me in so long. I had started to feel like a ghost. It wasn't against the rules to go down.

He touched my hip to guide me off the ladder into a mucky little stream. It smelled like shit. "It's slippery," he said, in the same tone he'd used to tell me to look up.

He was close to me now, like how we'd been the first time. The water swirled around us both. He touched the crinkled flesh around my eye sockets. "They hurt you so bad." His fingers traced the jagged rims. "It's my fault. I did this to you."

He reached in, stroking the inside of my eye socket. I could feel his fingerprints scraping into the red flesh close to my brain.

It felt like a violation. I jerked away. "How did they catch us? You said they never checked."

"You want to feel what they did to me?"

He took my hand and guided it into his pants, like I'd tried to do that first night. I wormed my hand down and there was nothing there. A purse-drawn blank. I jerked back at first, but then I reached back in, cupping the space between his legs. "Can you feel anything?"

"Not there."

"Why didn't they just do the eyes or hands thing?"

"Sometimes they get creative."

I kept my hand there, but I wasn't really moving it anymore. "What are we doing down here?"

"It's just – you could still be happy, right?"

"It's not really my thing."

"It's everybody's thing. It's just how far you gotta dig to get to it. I had to watch you, you know? I had to be sure you were cool. But listen for a sec, okay?"

"All I hear is water."

"No, past that. Hear the beat?"

I could. A thumping, faintly through the tunnels. A rhythm.

"You hear? This is where all of us come. As deep as we need to be. Everyone's missing something down here." I pulled my hand out of his pants and he held it in his. It was still clammy, but I let him do it.

We sloshed down the tunnel, through the water. Damp, spongy objects bobbed against my ankles. The music was getting louder, and I wanted it. I imagined secret scarred bodies pressing against each other, writhing together, down in these buried places.

But I imagined other things, too. The glint on the doctor's glasses. The scalpel. "If they catch me again..."

"Scary, right?" he said, and his fingers came up around my eye sockets again. "That's what makes it good. That's the only time I feel something. It makes me happy."

We came up several stairs to a door. It felt heavy and metal under my touch. Behind it was the music, a wild and insistent throbbing. I tried to open it, but it was locked.

"Pick a hand," said Ray. I reached out, fumbling through the air until I found one. It was empty.

"Pick the other one," he said, and guided me to it. There was a big iron key in it.

"I knew it," he said. "You're still choosing. There's still so much of you left."

The music sounded echoey through the door. I would have thought it would be absorbed into all those waiting bodies. I fumbled with the key. "Can't they hear the bass up there, though?" It was a heavy lock, but finally I turned it over and Ray reached around me to grab the handle.

"Of course they can," he said, and pushed it open.

■

Sasha Brown is a Boston writer, gardener and dad. His surreal fiction is here or coming in lit mags like X-R-A-Y *and* Masters Review: New Voices, *and in genre mags like* Old Moon Quarterly *and* F&SF. *He's on twitter* @dantonsix *and online at sashabrownwriter.com.*

GIVE THEM NO QUARTER, TELL THEM ALL LIES

———————————— ■ ————————————

Rebecca Bennett

Along the rocky coast of Newfoundland, Lindsay's imagination runs as loose as her tongue, loose as the pebbles that dig into her balding leather shoes. As loose as the morals she claims to have sacrificed to the sea. "Tell them," she whispers into the dusk. "Tell them I poisoned the crew. I slipped it into the rum, let them all drink. I laughed while their lungs bubbled into the air."

She squeezes the partridgeberries, small round and ripe, gathered just this morning into her fist. Feels each berry burst and stain before tossing the gritty red jam into the ocean foam.

"What color were the lungs?" Shark asks. Their voice swims in the air, nothing permanent in the tone to mark it one way or another. It could be curiosity or boredom. It's placid, calm like Eric's voice rarely is.

Lindsay thinks to the chickens she's gutted, to the carcass displayed at the butchers. Red is obvious. But she's already used red in the story, describing how she would have stabbed the first mate and used a red scarf to muffle the screams as she reached into his wounds. "Pink." She settles on. The poison would have foamed white and the lung's blood would have shifted to a murky pink at the contaminant.

"I found some bodies up the water," Shark says.

Everything is up the water to Shark. "Near the bay or further around?"

Ships didn't often wreck in the Gulf of Lawrence, but those that did—those that veered too close to the rocky ledge of Hibb's Cove—Lindsay claimed as her own. From the warm waters of the Caribbean to the docks in Port aux Basques, the name Maria Lindsay was becoming feared. A ruthless pirate who stalked these barren French waters. The Royal Navy, the Spanish Main, even privateers, were all said to have met the end of her merciless blade.

Shark found the wrecks and made sure the sailors knew the name. The one Lindsay held dear since she was young, playing by herself, dreaming up another person—

Maria—who would take charge in a way Lindsay never could. Maria didn't fear the vast water, she never married the first boy who asked.

"Thereish." Shark waves a webbed hand to the beach nearby. Lindsay twists as though a sailor has appeared, half-drowned and ready to hang her for her lies. There's laws against piracy, but Lindsay's not sure there are laws against pretending to be one.

"Should I be concerned?" Lindsay asks, this part of their friendship is new. She's unsure the lengths Shark will go beyond spreading the tale of Maria Lindsay, the mad pirate who gave no quarter in these remote waters. Whispering tales to drunken or drowning sailors is one thing, protection from half-dead men is another.

"No survivors from the wreck, if that's what you mean. I guess the poison didn't take to three of the men."

"Hmm." Lindsay shifts to a boulder closer to the water, not caring seawater is inching up her skirt, soaking her woolen socks. "What did I do then?"

Shark titters, whiskers twisting before answering. "Maybe you ate them?"

"Probably not. Can't eat bones, remember?" Sometimes Shark gets confused between bones and cartilage. Doesn't understand if Lindsay has sharp teeth why she can't just gnaw through. "Three you say? Hmm, maybe I dragged those three back to the beach. To make an example of them."

The remnants of *The Prudent* have been drifting onto the shoreline for the past few days. Splintered hull fragments touching land while its crew no longer could. The pieces were claimed quickly, townspeople looking for strong oak for their own houses. Shark is anchored to a floating section from the keel, the wood scrap is thick with black slime and armoured with barnacles. It knocks against the rocks that Lindsay keeps balanced on.

Shark's black eyes are focused only on Lindsay as they bob along the water in time with Lindsay's words. They'd been teaching the types of ships that Shark liked to feed from. Bodies drop so often over the sides of ships, Shark just travels along until their stomachs are filled for the winter. Lindsay looks at the size of the hull, guesses at the amount of crew and guns aboard, the riches being shuffled between three warring nations, and thinks that the ship might have been a schooner. Merchant probably, not military.

Shark has no lips, just rows of dark bristles that cover ladders of teeth. The wiry hairs flutter into what Lindsay thinks is a grin. "I'll leave you a gift tomorrow then. At dawn."

It's as much of a cue to leave as Shark is willing to give. The water has been lapping at Shark's thick waist, high tide creeping further up the folds of blubber that keep Shark warm as winter nears. They spend so much of their time in silence, Shark rarely speaking unless Lindsay has a story to weave into something grand.

When she leaves, Shark is just a pair of black eyes glinting in the night.

The next morning, Lindsay shuffles down to the beach. Wrapped in Eric's sweater and cap, her dark hair bundled underneath. The gift is laid out on the shore, three human heads. The skin mottled, bloated and sagging away from the bone. Seagulls pocket the sand, one or two swooping overhead before coming down to peck at the decaying meat. Lindsay doesn't wave them away, just watches the water recede further with low tide.

There's spawn on the water, floating even when the waves break. It's different from the frog spawn that accumulates in the spring. This belongs to Shark. It glows like pearls and Lindsay feels an echo of its frothiness deep within. *Yearning*—is the word that comes to mind. She met a sailor in Plymouth, before she and Eric moved to this new land, who swallowed whiskey like it was milk.

His right arm had been damaged in a wreck, the limb whole but unable to make a fist or hold a spoon. Had it just been cut off, he said, he could still be out on the water. *There's places for men like me out there, men that society would rather ignore.* He settled instead next to a port to watch the boats, so he could hear the call of the sea even though he couldn't meet it.

Yearning he called it. For the water, for the freedom.

She never yearned for Eric, maybe he never did either, and that's why it was so easy for them to hurt each other.

Lindsay yearns now. As the sunrise glows upon the spawn, she thinks of Shark laying those eggs, how some will grow into more creatures who will hunt and take stories from dying men. She wants to lay down among the eggs, feel the texture on her skin. It would change her, she thinks, just as Shark did.

They met in March when ice floats were still puddling on the water.

Shark had been a shadow under the current as Lindsay walked further and further into the waves. The cold waters of Hibb's Cove stole her breath before the water even reached her knees. There were icebergs among the waves, she should have expected the cold. She stood for hours, stillness turning to shaking, as she hoped for a riptide—something strong that would take the option from her. Just as her family did. Just as her husband did.

Standing still only ever gave rise to Lindsay being led, instead of leading. Without moving herself or being pushed forward, she ended up back on land, feet bleeding from the rocky beach and cracked mollusks.

Shark appeared just as Lindsay was bandaging her legs. The shaking had turned into fine tremors that didn't feel so cold anymore, and she thought it might be nice to lay down and nap before returning home. She was just about to do so when she caught the black glinting eyes.

"I see you," Lindsay chattered out, teeth clacking even though she swore she wasn't cold.

Shark leveled their head above the water, rising just enough that Lindsay could see the bristles along their dark mouth. "I see you, too."

Hail keeps the beach abandoned for two days. Lindsay imagines each head encased in ice, crystalized and shining. She wonders if she tapped them, if each head would shatter perfectly. The thaw comes and with it the discovery, finally noticed by a child looking for mussels.

The village comes to life once the heads are recovered. Each new trip to town brings new gossip that Lindsay lets warm her.

"Harvey heard that it's that *woman* again." The miller's wife, flour on her cheeks, bright and breathless. "Godless heathenness, what if my Ernie had been on that ship."

"Tooth marks on the necks, like the others." Moody rumbles, one eye on his pitcher of ale the other watching the sea. "I seen her ship, only ever appears in the fog."

"My brother met her once," the bartender says as he pours Eric another drink. "He was on the HMS Feversham, barely survived. He spent days on the water before being rescued. Told everyone about the woman who single-handedly sunk that warship. Brass shipped him right back to England."

Lindsay is pushed close to her husband's side. The stink of a day's work clings to his skin, wood shavings and body odor. Eric barks out a laugh. "A woman? Please, one trip to port and she'll be laid up on her back."

"It'll be winter soon, access will close up right quick. Won't need to worry about pirates until spring."

Hibb's Cove is a port town, every family has a sailor. Every family has stepped onto a boat and learned to move with the water rather than fight against it. There are people who read the weather better than the Bible, able to notice how a shift in the wind could mean sudden frost or storm. Lindsay has only felt that kind of attunement since meeting Shark. She knows, at the base of her spine, when Shark is nearby. Knows when Shark is amused or annoyed before they even break the surface.

She doesn't know Eric like that. Every move startles and chafes. He wears at her like sodden wool, heavy and clinging. They return to their tiny shack, Eric stumbling and loud enough that Lindsay can barely hear the crash of the waves. She lights a fire and begins cleaning the mussels she collected earlier. While Eric laughs about a female pirate ransacking their waters, she runs her hands along the shells, sliding her fingers into the crevices, touching the small sprigs of moss at the edges.

Shark's skin is similar to the eels that Lindsay sometimes catches. Their skin is mottled gray, blending into the rocks below the water. Instead of feet, there are two dorsal fins. Along the fins are tears and scars that have turned the slick skin craggy. Lindsay had been allowed to drag her hand across the surface once, feeling the hard matte skin beneath the algae coating Shark's body.

• • •

"Do you remember the Feversham?" Lindsay's crouched on the shore, idly picking up shells and flinging them into the water. Shark is beached next her to, looking up at the gray sky while water laps at their fins.

"Your boats have too many names," Shark answers. "Tell me again."

They've shared so much, but each lie is still so easy to pick out. Lindsay never stops telling stories, keeping them running in her head all day. "That was the British warship from the summer. It was headed to New France. We decided I found them while a storm raged. I landed on board and they didn't even hear me, not with all the rain."

Shark cocks their head. "You hanged the captain from the mast. Disemboweled the first mate. Took him all day to die."

Lindsay nods. It was one of the first stories she told. "Later, you found a sailor on the water, told him the truth of what happened."

"That took all day." Shark says. "He didn't want to believe it. Kept talking about the storm. He saw the truth in the end."

"Thank you." Lindsay wants to reach out, stroke her hand along Shark's flank. She doesn't, they don't like being touched out of the water and she has only ever wanted Shark to be happy.

There's a chill in the breeze that they aren't talking about. That they haven't talked about for days. The snow is falling steadily at night, now lasting for most of the day instead of melting by noon. The Gulf of Lawrence will freeze up and Shark will leave. They spoke about it before, when they first met and Lindsay wanted to know everything. If she asks, she makes it real. If she doesn't ask, Shark might just leave without telling her. Shark doesn't understand Lindsay's need to know and plan, they don't live according to England's time.

"When will you leave?" It hurts just to ask. She only thinks about the empty beach, inaccessible and dangerous with winter's ice. Lindsay will spend the season frozen in time within her shack. Cleaning and cooking and doing everything she can to keep warm. The room will stink of mildew and damp human bodies. There won't be wrecks or spawn or dark eyes. Just cold lonely evenings with Eric.

"Perhaps tomorrow, or the day after. It's a hard swim," Shark says. "My children will lay dormant under the ice, some will live. Some won't."

Lindsay's body has never successfully held a baby. She knows how easy it is to take and then lose. Shark faces it so easily, birthing hundreds only to see one or two live. It's rare for Shark's species to survive even to adulthood. Shark is not the only one of their pod to seek out humans, but they are the only one to return so often.

"When the ice melts and the water warms again, I'll return," Shark says before they leave. "I'll carry your name with me, let them know your deeds."

Maria Lindsay sets fire to a ship, listens to the men as they jump into the water. Choosing to drown rather than burn.

Maria Lindsay cuts the hands off three sailors and makes them row to shore.

Maria Lindsay steals thousands of Spanish real from a galleon. She buries her wealth on Groais Island, noting the location with a secret code.

Maria Lindsay kills her husband.

Over the winter, Lindsay keeps up her stories and butchers her way through their chickens and rabbits, becoming accustomed to the grind of bone under her blade. She holds their necks and slices straight through.

Eric keeps to bed. One day he starts coughing, his face red with fever. He tells her to go into town for the doctor. She lets herself stand still enough that she can hear the cracking of the ice flows. Doesn't bundle up in coats and blankets to walk into town. Doesn't go to Eric's side. She stands and waits.

Each week she chooses one chicken. Carves her path out to the coop, the lantern providing enough heat and light that Lindsay could wait outside for hours while Eric stays in bed. The flakes twist in the air, the wind gusting snow piles from the fences to the shack.

If she keeps standing, it's like the world is moving around her.

She wakes to the thunder of splintering ice. The ocean is groaning and shrieking as the ice dams melt and crack. The world is shifting; it's violent even without Maria Lindsay there to take her blood price. Eric is cold in bed next to her and she tells him a new story. She tells him about a ship, French this time, and how she rammed into the heart of it. Water rushing in like a spring thaw. Wood breaking apart like icebergs. She tells him how she smiled when she watched it sink.

Lindsay has thought about the first time she met Shark. If she had chosen to slip under the water, would they still be friends? Would Shark tell stories to a frozen Lindsay or would Shark have gnawed on her bones, feeding until Lindsay Cobden became a part of them?

Another week and she hears the waves again. Crashing onto the shore, calling her out to greet them. The path down is still slick with melting ice and snow, but she makes it. Steadfastly walking to where she hopes Shark will be waiting.

A patch of fresh spawn floats near the beach, the pearlescent foam popping as it tilts against the hard surface of rock and ice. It glows above the dark water and Lindsay thinks she can smell it in the breeze. She can feel Shark calling to her, it warms her core and she knows she cannot go another moment without answering their greeting. It's more than a want or desire, it's a needful thing that cannot be denied.

She walks into the frigid water, letting it chill her bones, and lays down among the spawn.

▪

Rebecca writes speculative fiction with small town flair. Her short stories and poetry have been published in Strange Horizons, Bourbon Penn, Translunar Travellers Lounge, *and other literary locations. She wields minor power as a Senior Editor at* Apparition Lit *and Managing Editor at* Heartlines Spec. *You can follow her occasional tweets at @_rebeccab*

THE FISHERMAN'S WIFE'S SON

Matthew Finn

The doctors arrive twenty minutes early, one elderly, one distractingly young, both in crisp white coats befitting their station, like doctors imitating the doctors on TV. I serve green tea and an expensive spread of rice crackers from Isetan, each bearing, I hope, this unspoken message: This is my life, dignified, considerate, same as yours. They are joined by a hulking, stone-faced assistant toting two black leather bags, and a silent nurse, nearly as large, inscrutable behind her white fabric surgical mask. We sit and chat awkwardly for several minutes on my living room floor, crowded around the low table of untouched crackers and rapidly cooling tea.

"Shall we begin?" the older doctor finally suggests, mercifully.

Let's.

I allow them to strap me to the bed to calm their nerves, though I'm not convinced that they should be the nervous ones.

"So you have complete control of this thing," the younger doctor wants to confirm as he snaps on a pair of eggshell latex gloves. "The thing submits to your will."

"And by 'the thing' you mean my own body," I say without malice. "By 'the thing' you mean me." I'm not sure how else to respond. He lets the inquiry go.

When they are all four gloved and masked, the older doctor nods to his burly assistant who reaches across the bed and slides my pants down over my hips, stopping at the knees. He steps away and there's the usual moment of stunned silence, disgust and awe. I look from one face to the next around their wide-eyed circle, then around again, like ticks on a clock. Time passes.

"The equipment," the older doctor commands, snapping them all back into the moment.

A sheen of sweat shimmers on the nurse's forehead as she busies herself with one of the black leather bags. She unzips and removes one instrument after another, perching them like steeled vultures along the ledge of my dresser, a grim assembly of cold silver edges and digital displays. I close my eyes as their examination begins. Their voices soon thicken to murmur, then fade completely as I retreat to my place, which is not really a place at all.

"The Genesis Memory," my dearest Miu once labeled it, as I struggled to describe it to her, Miu's head resting on my chest in a Dogenzaka love hotel. It always begins with a heartbeat: a thumping liquid pulse as if I am listening under water. The world is bathed in a soft red glow, like the warmth of sunlight through closed eyelids. It's tempting to believe the heartbeat is my own, but it's not. I know this because we always part. Some bond is severed and I'm ripped away.

So I hold on, cling desperately for as long as I can until, first softly, then sharpening, the doctors' voices return and I'm back in the apartment, strapped to my bed. They have finished and are disinfecting their instruments. They loosen my restraints and retreat back into the living room.

The damp sheets smell of sweat and alcohol. I sit up and pat my face dry with one end of a towel as my harassed organ pat pats with the other. Then it tugs up my pants and I join the doctors in the next room.

"More tests will be performed back at the lab," the older doctor says. "We'll evaluate the results and figure this thing out. But you have nothing to fear. We'll get you fixed, get you normal, living a normal life. You will be a functioning member of society."

I thank the doctors and see them to the door.

Back in the living room I return the crackers to their box. I dump the tea down the sink, then wash the ceramic cups, placing them one by one upside down in the drainer. They are beautiful things, a gift from Miu, purchased at an artisan's shop in Kamakura. Each is unique, hand formed, exquisitely painted with a fine ox-hair brush. I stare at the glistening wet cups for several minutes. Then, against my will, I cry.

My eyes are barely dry before another knock at the door and I know it's my neighbor Taka. The building's walls are thin and he hears everything. He always gives me a moment to compose myself before he arrives bearing his usual salve: two packs of Mild Sevens and a dozen jars of Cup Sake. He has a bag of wasabi chips and a bag of kaki-peanuts, the ever-present sketch pad tucked under his arm, and two pencils, as always, one behind each ear.

"Details!" he demands as he hands over the chips and sake. "I want big busty nurses and leather restraints, anal defilements for the advancement of Science." We sit on the tatami floor and he opens his sketch pad and begins to scribble, his scarlet, acne-pitted face a mask of concentration. There's already a page and a half of drawings imagined through the wall: the doctors cowering in the corner, me strapped to the bed raising a scalpel in one engorged tendril as a second wraps the nurse's thigh, disappearing up her short skirt.

"I won't let those bastards chop you, my fellow faux-functioning sub-member of society."

I twist open two sakes and we toast nothing but their being in our hands on another starless night.

"What if they hack off your cock and you die, but your cock, as the real you, survives?"

This is Taka's "What if?" game. It's how he generates plots for his manga.

"What if that's who you actually are? Your sentient core? And they dump you in an aquarium, a tourist attraction amid hostile, dead-eyed mollusks, or worse yet, smuggled away, a curiosity in a slime-green tank in a sushi shop window in the back alleys of Nihonbashi?" He sketches furiously: a bug-eyed dishwasher with a towel draped over his shoulder peers into a fish tank and pokes at cock-me with a chopstick.

"Then I won't be able to hurt anyone else," I say. "Problem solved."

He stops drawing but does not look up. "You're not the monster in this story." He shakes another cigarette from the pack and lights it. "Remember that."

If I'm not the monster, I'm tempted to ask, would we even be friends?

Taka hasn't ventured more than a hundred meters from his own front door since I've known him. He sneaks down to the mailbox to deliver his work and crosses the street to the convenience store to stock up on essentials—sake, chips, cup ramen, cigarettes—handling his banking at the ATM, but all of this only between the hours of three and four in the morning, and only when the store is completely deserted, to be ascertained through prolonged and patient surveillance. Despite being neighbors, we never would have met if he'd had the least indication that it was possible.

It was during the summer of chaos, the electrified dawn of my romance with Miu, when even alone in my room I could not sleep with clothes on. My very skin seemed to tear at itself, restless and inflamed with need. Every night I'd pull on thin cotton shorts only to find them tossed to the floor come morning, sometimes hidden beneath a pillow or behind the nightstand. Once, when I'd had the temerity to tie my shorts with a drawstring, I woke to the pair shredded to tatters, the drawstring looped menacingly about my neck in a makeshift noose. Day and night my mind was on Miu. Night and day, my body was in riot.

At half-past three that fateful morning, after twenty minutes at his peephole waiting for a drunk to put down a magazine and vacate the convenience store, Taka opened his door and scurried down the landing. He rushed down the darkened stairwell, taking the stairs two at a time. Just four steps from the bottom he landed on me. I was deep in sleep, stripped naked and slinking down.

It was not sleepwalking, to be precise. More of a sleep-drag—a series of extensions, find a purchase then pull. It was normal in those days to wake on the floor of my apartment, under the table, or in the kitchen affixed like a magnet to the refrigerator door. But that was the first time I'd ever made it outside, and if not for Taka's accidental intervention, there's no telling where my night may have ended. Taka guesses Miu's place. I posit the morgue.

Taka tumbled the final few steps to the bottom, then sprang to his feet, prepared to sprint. Desperate for the safety of his apartment, he caught a pre-flight glimpse of his obstacle, me, pantless, stunned and squirming in the damp night air. He recognized a being as freakish and malformed on the outside as he felt within. He saw in me a potential ally in this bitter world: a fellow outcast and long longed-for only friend.

And what if Taka is right? What if I had slunk all the way to Miu's place that night? Would everything have changed?

The sake is gone, Taka's sketch hand is cramping, and my brain is dribbling lethal thoughts like an acid-soaked sponge. I check the landing for signs of life. There is none, and Taka sneaks home.

The jars are in the sink and the ashtrays empty when there's another knock and I wonder what Taka has forgotten. I pull open the door to a stout woman in tight black jeans and a white sweater so fuzzy she appears vague, soft and nebulous as an oncoming cloud.

"I'm very sorry," the woman says, "but I had to talk to you alone. May I come in?"

It's after 4 a.m. and I'm not sure if this woman is lost, deranged, or merely drunk.

"They will kill you," she says. "And not one of them will give a damn." She glances down at the empty street and dabs sweat from her milky forehead with a small towel and I suddenly place her. It's the nurse from that afternoon, in a change of clothes and sans mask.

"And do you imagine I would?" I ask her.

"Let me in?"

"Give a damn, if they kill me."

The question rattles her and I grip the doorknob, not sure what I'm waiting for.

"My name is Yumi," she says, her painted lips quivering. "May I please come in?"

"I'm very sorry, Yumi." I push the door closed. "It's safer if you do not."

Miu was the most stunning bride I had ever seen. Just twenty years old, in a pure white kimono, hair sculpted into the divine geometry of a nautilus shell, in photo after photo, eyes ablaze with the inexorable radiance of youth and hope. The groom, a sergeant, two decades her senior, wore his police dress blues and stared down the camera like it was suspect in a heinous crime. In truth, it was merely witness.

They purchased a two-bedroom condo in a Harumi tower with a view of Rainbow Bridge and the glimmering distant lights of the bay. The sergeant had the second room converted to a nursery and painted a pale blue. After the first childless year of marriage, the pressure was on. After just two, the abuse began. Miu studied the calendar and tracked her temperature and diet with a scientist's rigor. The sergeant came home less frequently and less sober. The beatings grew steadily worse.

By twenty-six, Miu had lost eight kilos and all hope. She barely ate and rarely left the house, her wrists now ribbed with a thin ladder of self-cut scars. She ghosted the internet or stared out over the bay at the distant threads of light, occasionally taking scrupulous phone messages from her husband's more brazen mistresses. Alone on the night of her seven-year wedding anniversary, she registered on a forum under the screenname "whatsmiu." She'd made a plan but wanted to be certain it would work.

It would work, our virtual pharm experts agreed; the dosage would be more than enough. It would take less than twenty minutes, and she wouldn't feel any pain.

"Godspeed Miu," I joined in chorus. How I wish now I would have stopped writing then.

The next evening, Taka arrives at my door with a half-dozen pages devoted to my pre-dawn rendezvous with the nurse, Yumi. He'd listened through the wall. His sketchbook is beginning to read like my unauthorized biography, but he never apologizes for the intrusion.

How's he to discern, he asks, the many voices rising from within his own head from the precious few rising from without? It's an impregnable defense.

The series begins moments after I closed the door.

Panel 1: Crosscut of Yumi and I separated by the door. Her fingertips brush the outside right where my forehead is resting within.

"A bit melodramatic," I protest to Taka.

"Are you claiming that your forehead was not pressed mournfully to the door?" he asks.

I'm not.

Panel 2: A close-up of Yumi's large eyes, moist with tears. "I know what happened to Miu," she says to the closed door. "I know the truth. I know what the newspapers couldn't print."

Panel 3: Close-up of me, eyes squeezed shut, a man fighting back the demons of memory.

Panel 4: "Miu loved you," Yumi says, searching for just the right words. "You gave her a reason to live. What happened after doesn't change that."

Panel 5: Me, shattered. I unlock the door and pull it open a crack. "Are you married?" I ask Yumi.

This last line strikes me as morbidly slapstick and I tell Taka so.

"I agree," Taka says, "but those were your exact words."

Yumi promised me she wasn't married and I let her in. The following panels progressively enmesh.

The series ends with a single full-page image of our apartment building from outside. There is a man in a long coat standing in the shadows beside the convenience store. He grips a cellphone in one hand and looks up at the darkened building with its one lit window, my room, aglow from within.

"Why did you draw this man?" I ask Taka.

"Because he was there."

The newspapers couldn't report what they were not allowed to know. That Miu had been over an hour and a half late. That I'd rushed to greet her when my doorbell finally rang. That I was met by the sergeant with a police-issue duffel bag slung over one shoulder.

"What can I do for you, officer?" I'd asked, struggling to wrangle my voice.

He drew his service revolver and smashed the butt against my temple.

"Just be yourself," he'd said as I writhed on the floor. "And I'll be me."

The sergeant gripped me by the hair and dragged me into the kitchen, the linoleum floor squealing beneath his polished black boots. He opened the cupboard under the sink and cuffed my wrists together around the drainpipe.

"We haven't met, but I believe you know my wife."

The duffel slammed on the countertop with a metallic clatter. I heard the zipper, the sergeant's rummaging, then he knelt beside me with a stubby curve-backed blade.

"Do you know what this is?"

It was an Ikasaki, a fisherman's knife specially designed for breaking down squid. I've no idea what subconscious murk this knowledge sprang from. "A squid knife," I said.

The sergeant was so delighted with my answer he repeated it aloud. "Yes! A squid knife!" he said, full of mirth. "Now we're going to see if all these fish tales are true."

In her diary, I'd later learn, Miu had struggled for adjectives to match her enthusiasm for my anatomy. Her creative efforts bounded from "voracious" to "prehensile," from "multi-tasking" to "empathetic." The sergeant must have shaken his head at the twisted depths of his wife's fantasy world.

But what to make of the mounting evidence that had driven him to find her diary in the first place? Miu was suddenly back to a healthy weight. She'd let her hair grow out and even had it styled. She was leaving home, daily. Something was wrong. She seemed happy. It was time to investigate.

The sergeant had my ankles pinned beneath his knee. My pants were down and he held the knife to the base of my cock. He'd had to swap the Ikasaki for a larger blade. We were both now mirthless.

"You haven't cared about Miu in seven years. Why start now?"

"This will hurt," he said. "You'll pass out from the pain, but I have tools to staunch the bleeding and bring you around. Don't worry, you won't miss a thing, the party has just begun."

"Help! Police!" a shrill voice screamed out. It wasn't my own.

The sergeant spun, knife raised, expecting someone else in the apartment, just as Taka launched a hellbent assault against his own kitchen wall. He hurled a relentless stream of pans and dishes, kicks and profanities, even the odd limp fist dinging the drywall. The cacophony was dizzying.

Eyes shut, hands still cuffed, my anatomy rose, voracious, prehensile. It lassoed the sergeant's wrists and neck. I squeezed.

"Are you okay?" I called out to Taka when it was over.

I could hear his hoarse sobs through the battered wall. He'd never been in a fight before. "I'm fine," he said, "but I can kiss my security deposit goodbye."

The sergeant was lying across my lap, wide-eyed, still. I hadn't choked him to death. I'd crushed his larynx and severed his brainstem.

The police didn't ask me a single question that first week; they beat me with long sticks and bowled me into walls with a high-powered hose. They'd lost one of their own, and guilty or not, someone had to pay. But none of them were willing to touch me for fear of contagion. The first doctors to study me arrived in bright orange hazmat suits.

After ten days, tempers cooled and the official interrogation began. The story didn't make any more sense to them than it did to me.

"So, you met Miu on an internet forum where members help each other commit suicide."

"Plan suicide."

"Then neither of you killed yourselves. Instead, you met for coffee and fell madly in love. Didn't this somehow violate forum rules?"

"We met for tea."

"Were you both banned from the website for life?"

For twenty-four hours the police had been unable to contact Miu to inform her of her husband's death. When they entered the condo they found her naked, cuffed to the top of the dining room table. She'd been sliced open from breast to pelvis. Eviscerated. A limp dead octopus placed in her mouth.

"Did you know that Miu kept a diary?"

"I did not."

"And what about the news in the diary?" The detective paced the room with Miu's notebook in hand. He flipped through the final pages of her life, pinning cause to effect, knowing from the beginning only how it would end. "Did Miu ever happen to mention that she was carrying your spawn?"

As days became weeks, innocence unequivocal, the interrogation flowed inevitably to negotiation. The real story was never to get out. They'd released a revised version for the media, polished and suitable for public consumption. No cock-monster vs psychopathic rogue cop, but a lovers' quarrel ending in tragedy. It was an easy enough fiction to maintain. The police were forced to admit that I'd done them a favor in dispatching the sergeant. It would be far more complicated if he were still alive. Now they were hoping I'd tie up one final loose end. Me.

If I were awaiting trial, the detective informed me, I'd be on suicide watch. But as things stood, technically, I was a free man. They held me in a windowless concrete cell equipped with an eye hook in the ceiling, a metal stool and coil of nylon rope.

I hung a noose and paced the cell, haunted by the most painful memory of them all: sitting on a flat rock overlooking the sea. Holding Miu in my arms. Her warmth. Her smile. The scent of her hair.

"Promise me," she'd said. "Then I will promise you." She looked right into my eyes. She must have known on that day that she was pregnant with my child.

"I promise." My fingers traced her scarred wrists like a man memorizing his holy text in braille. It was too easy to say, just to hear her say it back. "I promise you, my love. I will never kill myself."

I agree to meet Yumi again in a basement coffee shop in East Shinjuku: a dozen battered tables in a plume of smoke trussing a dozen battered men as chimneys. She's wearing her fabric mask, sunglasses, and a second skin of makeup layered thick as a crepe. She hands me an envelope of photographs from China, Russia, Belarus.

"And this is the world you want me to hold out for?" I ask her, scanning the photos. Beneath the table I contract, ill at ease.

When the focus first shifted from a radical STD super-conflagration to a standard—if abhorrently formed—Siamese-twinning, it was a welcome development for all parties involved. I was not the discarded son of a hyper-syphilitic sailor and gonorrheic-herpetic port-whore. I wouldn't be managed by chemical cocktail. I'd be placed under the knife. It would be a risky procedure, the new doctors informed me. They couldn't guarantee survival. The police had given up tailing me once they realized I was an easy out. I just couldn't do it alone. Now they finally found someone to step up and catch the damned ball. I imagined them all high-fiving down at HQ. I was tempted to shake-shower in a bottle of champagne myself.

Yumi's envelope of horrors portrays similar procedures, all of them failed. The unloved and unwanted, human beings born lacking symmetry, the abnormal, stretched out on tables, sliced and disassembled to a grisly collection of component parts. Every patient was lost and every photo was exactly the same: uniquely indescribable.

"This is your future," Yumi tells me. "They're not trying to help you. They're trying to look like they tried."

"I appreciate the effort." I hand her back the envelope.

As she slides it into her bag, the sleeve of her blouse crawls up her plump pale wrist and I glimpse the jagged end of a scar, peeking out like the shiny purple head of a viper. She tugs her sleeve down immediately, instinctively, a cutter's reflex I recognize from Miu.

"You are a lovely woman, Yumi." I grasp her hand, suddenly overcome with an emotion I can't define. "You're beautiful, courageous, and I wish that I could know you under different circumstances, but I cannot."

Her hand trembles in mine, and mine over hers.

"You can't save me," I say. "I want this. I need this."

Yumi begins to cry, tiny swift streams trailing sediment of mascara.

"Check the forum," she says. "Login one last time and see what it's become. Then leave us, if it's what you must do."

I exit the coffee shop five minutes before Yumi. When I'd mentioned the man in the long coat outside of my apartment the night she visited, Yumi was undeterred, but we agreed to take precautions.

Out on the street I spot a black sedan halfway down the block, idling at the curb. The windows are tinted and I can't see who's at the wheel. I hope the car follows me. I hope they abduct me and drive to an industrial dock somewhere in Yokohama. I'll kneel at the edge before they even ask, let them put two slugs in the back of my skull and pitch me into the bay. Get this over with. I turn and walk slowly toward the station, looking back once. The black sedan remains at the curb.

I didn't check the forum, but apparently Taka did. He invites me over the next evening to preview his newest manga series in development. I bring the sake. He's flush with chips.

Taka's apartment is a mirror image of my own, but without the clean. Teetering stacks of manga climb every wall and there are at least five TVs visible from any given point, all of them on all of the time, muted and tuned to different stations. Research, he says. He doesn't go out into the world but must draw it from here. He stares at the silent screens for hours—so this is a nightclub, this twist of slime a snake-hatchling, and over there a mob hurls bottled fire at mounted police—each image another confirmation of his one deeply held belief: Do not fucking go out there.

"Imagine there are holes in this city," Taka says. We sit at his desk/draft board/kitchen table, a removed closet door covered with formica laid over two collapsable plastic sawhorses. He spreads his storyboard out. "Imagine descending into a subway station, mistakenly turning left instead of right, passing behind some random pillar, and just falling right through."

His drawings portray a Boschian nightmare realm, a darkened city under the city, peopled with the lost, frightened and lonely. They hug themselves, squatting in vast shadowy tunnels, or trudge knee deep through sewage, tapping out improvised codes on a long disused network of rusting pipes. They listen for signs of life from above, desperate to be remembered, to be missed, to be sought.

"So, your hero is going to patrol the city popping manhole covers, armed with a gaff?" I ask.

"The setting is more of a metaphorical backdrop."

"He'll scoop them out like guppies into streams of daylight and buckets of joy?"

"This is about the people. Survival. Holding on for something."

"I'm not sure if this is your most promising scenario."

"Everyone on that website is talking about you and Miu." Taka cuts to the point. "There are a lot of rumors about her death, the cover-up, about you, and most of them are true. They've taken a collective break from offing themselves. No more suicides. They're hooked on your story and sticking around to see where it goes."

"A statistical anomaly certain to confound social psychologists."

"This is a writer's biggest dream," Taka says. "After the fame and fortune and mountains of pussy, it's all about telling a story that can save lives. This is real."

I stare blankly at a random TV screen. A string of policemen duck under a ribbon of yellow tape. There's a voluminous chalk-figure sketched on a patch of bare pavement beside a weedy vacant lot.

I start to tell Taka the series might have a short run. My surgery is scheduled in three days' time. I open my mouth and he silences me with a raised palm. A few seconds later, I hear it too. Footsteps on the landing. A whisper, scraping, the creak of a hinge, my apartment door being forced open. We hear several people move stealthily through my kitchen and living room, then pause at my bedroom door. It slides open. "Shit," a voice says, sounding so close and clear it could be my own. "He's not here."

They move around the room for a few minutes, then the whole soundscape repeats in reverse. Taka pads silently to his front door and studies their departure through his peephole.

"Four men with guns. Look like gangsters with sensible shoes. Must be cops." He waves me over to see a lone car parked beside the convenience store. "One stayed behind to wait for you."

"I don't get it," I say.

"Well, you might want to crash here until you do," Taka says. "But I'm locking my bedroom door."

I wake hugging my knees on Taka's mini sofa, the walls flickering with televised light like a plugged-in Plato's cave.

"Have you ever had a chick and her mother on your noodles at the same time?" Taka asks from the kitchen.

"Of course not."

He breaks a raw egg into a styrofoam bowl of chicken ramen and brings it to me. "Then you're in for a real treat."

I eat and watch a familiar scene on TV. The same line of cops ducking under the same yellow police tape, the same chalk outline on the ground. It appears on another channel as well, and another, drawing the great collective consciousness to a point: News being made.

They flash two photographs on the screen, first a man, then a woman, and my stomach turns.

"Volume, Taka, volume!"

He grabs a remote and points it three ways before it takes.

The chalk outline, the murdered man, was the doctors' burly assistant, the muscle who'd strapped me down and lowered my pants. He was found last night, strangled to death. The woman, his coworker, is reported missing. The photo of Yumi is the same from her badge, sad-eyed and self-conscious in her nurse's uniform. The police have a suspect in the case. They show a photo of the suspect. The suspect is me.

"But I've done everything they've asked! Why kill the assistant? Why Yumi? Why frame me?"

"It would take a beast to strangle that man."

"I'm turning myself in."

"No, you aren't," Taka says. "Unless you miss the sticks and fire-hosing, we're getting you out of here. I have a plan." Then he promptly sits down and begins drawing manga.

Taka's plan is to out-surveil the surveillance. He spends the next four hours with his eye to the peephole. I set up on the sofa with five remote controls, casting for any news of Yumi.

"Ready, ready, ready, wait, wait, wait." Taka runs an endless stream of disconnected commentary, never explaining just what I should be ready or waiting for. I'm not ready for any of this—for Yumi's body fished from the bay, or another billowy chalk outline—but I wait, still.

"Ready, wait ... Go!" Taka says. And when I look up, he is gone.

His door slams and I hear my keys rattle, my door open, my door close, before I'm even on my feet. Taka is in my apartment and out of breath. "Man the peephole," he commands through the wall. "Look sharp. You'll know when it's time."

"Time for what?"

Taka crosses to my bedroom. A drawer slides open, then shut. He crosses back to the front door and I can feel his presence beside me on the other side of the wall. I hear him swallow. The acoustic quality startles me. "You can hear everything from here," I say. I'd never heard Taka this clearly from my side of the wall.

Outside, dawn is breaking. The cop emerges from the convenience store with a can of coffee, cigarettes and a curry roll. He goes back to the car, climbs in, lowers a window and lights a smoke.

"It looks like you're going to be trapped there for a while," I tell Taka.

"I hear every breath you take," Taka says. "Every pathetic, self-loathing sigh. I hear your heart beat, your brain tick, and I know that you masturbate with two hands, that you cry in your sleep, that you dream of death, and that these dreams bring you peace. And death will come for you someday, my friend. I promise that. But for now, you're going to have to wait for it like the rest of us." Then Taka opens the door and steps out onto the landing. He's wearing a sweatshirt from my drawer with the hood pulled up, a pair of sunglasses concealing his eyes.

The cop is nearly as shocked as I am. He scrambles for the radio, spilling his coffee across the console.

Taka is down the stairs and to the sidewalk in a flash. He sprints around the corner and out of sight before the cop is even out of his car. When the cop is around the corner, too, I step out onto the landing, go down the stairs, turn left instead of right, and disappear.

A block. A dozen blocks. Nothing changes.

The farther I get, the more lost, the more familiar the city becomes, until soon there is no curb or bench or alley I do not know. I stop at a staircase leading into a subway station I'm sure I've been to before, though I can't recall when or why. Then I place it: It's all from Taka's art, his sketches and manga. For a man who's spent his entire adult life in a room watching television, he's rendered this world with prophetic accuracy, and I'm no longer sure if the city I'm traveling has inspired his work, or if this is his work, sprung from the page and projected out onto the bare white walls of reality.

I rush down the staircase and trip, tumbling, spiraling, until I finally come to rest in a dark tunnel tide-marked in epochs of human waste. A malefic creek trickles along the floor and I know before I even look that a network of rusting pipes will twine overhead. I've reached the labyrinth: Taka's city under the city. My life has become the manga of my life.

I ran from the apartment because Taka had willed it, but I can never outrun this simple truth: If I'd died in jail, Yumi would be unharmed. If I'd lived differently, maybe Miu would, too.

I have crossed the zero border and entered an empty box. From here, I'll plot the end, and Taka will have no choice but to draw it as it is.

From a length of cord salvaged from the muck, a noose is fastened to the pipes overhead. This, Taka, is the final climb. But how could a single panel ever hope to depict the crush of guilt and great shrieking panic inside?

"My Miu, my Yumi, I am so sorry," the caption will read.

I release my grip on the pipe and swing into the void. Even as I choke them out, the words fall desperately short.

• • •

"Words fall short," the young widow says, "but sometimes they are all we've got." She sits cross-legged on the sofa in black jeans and a black turtleneck sweater, Taka's manga, my story, open on her lap. On the page there is an image of me in silhouette, hanging by the neck, unconscious.

"We read your words and we can understand," she says, "because we feel them. Because the pain they bear is also our own."

On the table there's a photo of her with her husband on their honeymoon in Izu. She leans into his chest. His arms wrap her shoulders. He was diagnosed with acute leukemia six months later, and dead seven months after that. He was twenty-four years old.

Ten days after her husband's funeral, after the flowers had wilted and the food-bringers and company-keepers had gone, she chased a dozen sleeping pills with half-a-bottle of shochu—anything to be with him again.

She turns the page and in the following panels we see a tendril stretch up and wrap the pipe, supporting my weight as another works the cord free. I woke on the ground, hours later, with a pounding head, caked in muck. The widow was gone twice as long. She'd woken alone, her stomach emptied on the bedroom floor. "The body saves the day," she says.

We drink green tea and talk and laugh until it's time to leave. Before we head to the police station, she wraps a scarf around my neck to hide the cord burns, though they're nearly gone. She places her hands on my face and kisses me softly. "We're not alone," she says as we walk out the door.

We're not alone. I'd stay with a truck driver, a cellist, a college drop-out, a retiree. From ten thousand forum members came ten thousand invitations, each offering a spare futon or sofa, space on the floor or space in bed. There were ten thousand stories, ten thousand listeners, and ten thousand activists, an army of us come together and committed to a single cause. Taka drew the plan. The plan would start with one.

A woman in black jeans and a black turtleneck sweater, the young widow, walks into the Shinjuku Police station just before noon.

"Yumi, the missing nurse, we know where she is," the widow says to the officer manning the reception desk.

He considers the proper combination of forms to offer. "Where?" he asks as he hands her two.

"Downstairs. In a cell." Then she hands him a manga: Tentacle Boy, Volume I. "Read this," she tells him. "Just so you know what we know."

The officer opens the manga to a bookmarked page. In the first sequence he sees a woman in black jeans and a black sweater walk into a police station claiming to know where Yumi is. "Downstairs. In a cell," the caption reads. Then she hands him a manga and leaves the station. On the street outside a crowd has gathered.

The officer looks up from the manga just in time to see the woman walk out the door and disappear into the gathering crowd. He lifts the receiver of the desk phone to call his commander. "Something's happening here," he says.

"What if this is real?" On the page, Taka is acne-free. He's standing beside a river and points straight out of the panel, straight at the reader. In manga form he appears to have packed on ten kilos of solid muscle.

"What if all those people you see outside are real?" the next caption reads. "What if their pain, their anger, is real? Then wouldn't the fear that you're feeling in your gut right now, as you read this, be 100% real? What would you do then? How would you proceed?"

The manga picks up Yumi's story outside the coffee shop where we'd met in East Shinjuku. We see her walking north up the street, the black sedan creeping behind. The car lurches ahead and cuts her off at the corner. A window slides down.

"Get in," the doctors' burly assistant says. Yumi does. He's always more dangerous when she says no.

Taka would illustrate the whole sordid history, from their first date, through the first signs of his instability and Yumi's rising fear, to her leaving him, or attempting to leave him, walking home from one nightmarish encounter bloodied and in tears.

He chronicles the stalking and threats that would lead to Yumi's first trip to the police, where she filled out a form. Then the attack that followed, his knife at her throat in the back seat of his car, and her second trip to the police where she'd fill out the same form. On her third visit, an officer suggested relationship counseling. On her fourth, she was led to a small private waiting room where she sat alone for three hours. Then a clerk brought her the familiar form.

Taka ends the sequence with Yumi's final trip to the police, weeks later, driving the dead assistant's black sedan. She'd gone home first, showered, slept, then shared her story with a few thousand trusted online friends before turning herself in: how she'd been abducted in Shinjuku and driven to a vacant lot in Yokohama. How she was forced into the back seat and stripped. And how, her tormentor lost in passion, she worked her torn blouse around his neck, slid behind, and squeezed. The assistant was strong. Yumi was stronger.

"We don't know exactly what you're thinking," Muscle-Taka admits from the following page, stalking the riverside, "but we do know how you think. You've made mistakes and now you want them gone, two birds, one dirty stone."

The next panel is a close-up of Taka's bloodshot eyes, fierce, enraged. "But we aren't going anywhere," the caption reads. "We in the margins are more than you think. We can lead and not follow. Take another look at the freaks outside. We are real, and unlike you, we have nothing to lose. Now turn the page to see exactly how you'll proceed..."

This could be any river. This is the river Taka drew.

I step out of my shoes and wade out until the water reaches my waist. It's a warm day, the sun high overhead, and small fish gather in my shade, pointing like thin silver darts upstream.

"That water can't be clean," Taka says from shore. He and Yumi sit in canvas chairs beside the tent. He's still not happy outdoors, but with Yumi by his side he can almost feign normal. "I have considered environmental factors of course: mercury, cesium-137, atomic even," he says. "Perhaps his father was a fisherman's brat dragged out on the Lucky Dragon #5, trawling the Bikini Atoll. He's freaky enough, but doesn't glow."

"I can hear you," I call from the water.

"But of course that tale has already been told," Taka says.

Taka is determined to write my origin story for Volume II, and has spent the past few weeks sketching possibilities.

"This print is entitled 'The Fisherman's Wife,'" he tells Yumi, showing her a reproduction of the 1814 woodblock print from the great ukiyo-e artist, Hokusai. In it, a woman lies naked on the sea floor as she's pleasured by a pair of octopuses. "Have you ever posed nude?" Taka asks Yumi. I wait for the sound of a slap, but hear only Yumi's delightful laughter.

The fish drift in close to my legs and do not struggle when tentacles wrap their slick charged bodies and pass them gently into my hands. I lift them from the water one by one for a flash tour of this world. "Look," I tell them. "There is the shore, there is the horizon, there is the city, and there the sky." Then I show them Yumi and Taka. "And those are my friends," I say. "I wouldn't be here without them. Or without the love of Miu."

The fish gawk and gape, tube-lipped, only half-believing, I'm sure, this dream world, this other side. But it's all true, and we're all here in it.

"Tentacle Boy, Volume II: The Fisherman's Wife's Son," I hear Taka announce from shore.

I can feel him watching me, sketching my every move. I feel the sweep of his wrist and hand, his pulse racing down through the pencil, informing each line.

"Remember this," I say as I lower the fish back into the world they know. "This is real," I tell them as they fin slowly from my hand, into the current and away.

■

Matthew Finn's stories have appeared in Gargoyle Magazine, Japanzine, *and* Crime Factory. *He grew up in Florida, and has lived in Reno, Nevada and Tokyo, Japan.*

THE STORY OF MY HOPES

---- ■ ----

Adrian Borda

My name is Borda D. Adrian, I'm a surreal painter and live in Reghin, Romania, the city where I was born on 21 nov 1978, a peaceful place with no social life, an ideal place to observe the artistic fight inside me. I started to take painting seriously when I went to high school, then I graduate fine arts in Iasi.

I'm an inner traveler, exploring the mysterious and extremely complex subconscious world. In my real life as well as in my art, I don't care about conventions and the taboos, there are no sacred memes that cannot be touched. My paintings are deep meditations full of symbols about life and out most intimate tendencies and reactions ... not necessarily to create something most people like, but to open a window to haunting images impossible to forget.

I've had some personal and group expositions in Romania at Targu-Mures, Iasi, Reghin, and Eindhoven in Netherlands. My works are in private collections all over the world, since I started selling on eBay: United States, Hungary, Canada, France, Switzerland, Japan, United Kingdom, Netherlands, Belgium, Greece.

THANK YOU!

PATREON SUPPORTERS:

Jer Blane

Daniel Gardner, HfB

Todd Gill

Elad Haber

Brent Jones

Anthony Notarfrancesco

Damon Savage

Peter T. Secker

Dave Sturgeon

Tony